SECRET NINJA SPIES

The black-clad figure raised its hands in challenge to the thugs, who growled and rolled up their sleeves.

"Yay! Go...mysterious ninja!" Jessica cried.

The figure executed a perfect spinning high kick to the first thug's face, sending him reeling. The second thug tried to grab hold, but their rescuer used his momentum to bounce the man's head off the wall.

Josh was stunned. This was a superhero. A real life, seriously for serious superhero had just rescued him!

SECRET NINJA SPIES

TOKYO SURPRISE

ALEX KO

USBORNE

First published in the UK in 2011 by Usborne Publishing Ltd., Usborne House, 83-85 Saffron Hill, London EC1N 8RT, England. www.usborne.com

Series created by Working Partners Limited.
Text copyright © Working Partners Limited, 2011
Illustrations copyright © Usborne Publishing Ltd., 2011
Illustrations by Kanako and Yuzuru.

The name Usborne and the devices ♀ 🌐 are Trade Marks of Usborne Publishing Ltd.

A CIP catalogue record for this book is available from the British Library.

ISBN 9781409515104 JFMAMJJASON/10 02335/1
Printed in Reading, Berkshire, UK.

Chapter One

"Tell me where you've hidden the device," Josh Murata demanded, facing his enemy as dust and broken glass settled around the devastated airport lounge.

Mr. Hamada laughed, his muscles bulging out of the torn sleeves of his shirt. "You cannot stop me, now."

Whooosh! Smack!

Josh sent his fist flying through the air and connected with Mr. Hamada's cheek.

Skeeeee!

Mr. Hamada's shoes skidded on the airport floor from the impact. But he recovered quickly and grabbed Josh's shoulders, throwing him.

CRASH!

Josh went through the final unbroken duty-free shop window, sending tiny fragments of glass spiralling. He raised his head to see Mr. Hamada sneering in triumph...

"Pardon me, Master and Miss Murata," said the red-skirted airline attendant. "We've got to go to the gate now."

"Huh?" Josh Murata said, looking up from his illustration.

The airport announcement bell chimed. "Passengers for the 10:35 Japan Jet flight to Tokyo, please assemble at Gate Three for boarding."

Josh's twin sister Jessica elbowed him and his pencil slipped, giving Mr. Hamada's sneering face an unfortunately gigantic nose.

"C'mon, we've got to go," she said, peering over his sketchbook, where the airport battle was laid out in six and a half comic book panels. "That looks cool," Jessica said.

"You see them?" Josh said, pointing across the lounge. Two Japanese men in black suits and sunglasses stood in the middle of the duty-free shops. One was short and fat and grey-haired, and the other looked like he had stepped out of the pages of a comic book – Josh had hardly needed to exaggerate the muscles at all. The two men were talking, leaning together as if they didn't want to be overheard. "They're clearly plotting something."

"Oh yeah," Jessica grinned. "They're going to go on a rampage any minute now. Just like Granny Murata's going to go on a rampage if we miss our flight."

"All right, I'm coming," Josh said, packing his pencil and sketchbook away.

They grabbed their backpacks and followed their appointed guardian's clicking high heels towards Gate Three. As they came up to the boarding area, Josh could see the plane through the big glass windows. It was one of the new double-decker ones with the red and black Japan Jet logo painted along the sides.

"Mum and Dad could have landed in Africa by now," Jessica said. "I bet they're saving lives already."

"Could be," Josh agreed. He could see them now, jetting into a war zone with only a surgeon's tools and a *Médicins Sans Frontières* van for protection. He felt a swell of pride. He was sure they'd be fine, but it was still a lot braver than anything most parents did. "I hope Granny's got some exciting stuff planned for us too. Anything other than listening to the history of the tea ceremony again!"

"I *like* the tea ceremony," Jessica said. "Anyway, last time we visited Tokyo, you spent all week in the bookstore drooling over manga you couldn't even read."

"Yeah, but it was research for my future career as a famous comic book artist. And anyway – *manga*!" Josh sighed happily, visualizing Granny Murata's local bookstore – shelves and shelves of the Japanese comics, more manga than he'd ever seen in one place. They had all the famous series he'd read in English plus hundreds never seen before...

Wham!

Josh walked head first into someone's back, and found himself looking up into the angry face of the huge Japanese man with the sunglasses.

The man shoved Josh away so hard that he stumbled and nearly ended up on the floor. It was like being pushed aside by the Incredible Hulk's angrier Japanese cousin. He gazed down at Josh from behind impenetrable black sunglasses. It was impossible to guess what he was thinking.

Josh swallowed hard, taking in the sheer size of the man. He was three times as wide as Josh and much taller. He straightened up to stand face-to-face with the man – though his head only came up to the man's enormous chest.

"*Kamawanaide Kure*," the man snarled, and he stomped off, resuming his mobile phone conversation.

"Shove off yourself," Josh muttered, brushing himself down.

"How rude!" Jessica exclaimed, helping Josh with his backpack.

Josh decided that the guy couldn't be an evil villain – he was too much of a thug. He was a lower-level henchman at best, one that would be killed off by the hero in the first scene.

"Doesn't matter," Josh said. "Let's get on the plane."

Their seats were on the top deck. Even on the

double-deckers, it was cramped. Josh nearly hit an old lady over the head with his backpack, and then had to dodge around a toddler that was dashing up and down the aisle chased by his frazzled mother. Finally they settled into their seats and Josh leaned his head against the window. As they took off, he watched the houses below shrink away to dots and disappear into the clouds.

The seat belt sign flicked off with a soft *bing*, and Jessica gasped. She was staring at something further up the plane, her eyes shining with excitement.

"Josh!" she hissed. "Look who it is!"

Josh looked. There was his new nemesis, standing at the curtained doorway to first class – the guy with the sunglasses.

"Oh great," he said. "We're on the same flight as that thug."

Jessica gave him a look of disbelief. "Are you *blind*? Look who he's talking to!"

Josh looked again. The man was talking to a very pretty Japanese girl, a little older than Josh, who was wearing a cropped high-fashion pink shirt, black jeans, and an amused smile.

"It's Kiki!" Jessica hissed. "Oh wow, we are sharing air with Chiba Mikiko! That man must be her bodyguard. I knew she was in London," she added, straining in her seat to get a better look, "recording English language tracks for her new album."

"Oh, *that* Kiki," Josh said, as Kiki and the bodyguard disappeared through the curtain into first class. "The pop idol with all those albums clogging up your iPod. She sang that song you've listened to every day for months about being in love with a cloud."

"It's *'Kumo no ue no ai'*, you idiot," Jessica said, still grinning. "'Love *On* The Clouds'." She took a deep breath and then dived into her bag and pulled out a notebook and pen. "I have to get an interview. Can you imagine Ellie Rowland's face when I get it onto the front page of the school paper? She'll just *die*."

"What?" Josh stared at Jessica. "No way. Kiki will never talk to you just like that. Anyway, she's in first class; you can't just wander up there."

"I *have* to – I've never been on the front page before." She unclipped her seat belt and stood up. "Get ready to cover for me when I give you the signal."

"Wait, Jess," Josh said. "Come back – *Jess!*" But it was too late. Jessica strolled off, while Josh sank lower in his seat and tried to look invisible, wondering whether anyone would believe him if he claimed not to know her.

A flight attendant came out of the midsection cabin, pushing the refreshment cart. Josh groaned. Jessica was going to have to squeeze past her to get into first class. He felt his heart pound harder with every step Jessica took. They were on course for collision…Josh raised his hand slowly towards the *Call Attendant* button on his seat, but it was too late…

"I'm Kiki's cousin," she said in a loud, confident voice, "can I just slip past?"

Unpleasant visions of both of them being taken down by Kiki's own personal Incredible Hulk danced before Josh's eyes. What happened if you got in trouble on an aeroplane? He imagined being handcuffed and forced to spend the rest of the journey in the hold.

The attendant raised her eyebrows at Jessica. Josh tried to beam a warning into the back of his sister's head by sheer force of concentration. *She's not buying it, Jess! Abort, abort!*

"What are you doing back here, if your seat is in first class?" the attendant asked.

"I've never been on a double-decker plane before," said Jessica. "I wanted to have a look around. Bored now."

The attendant hesitated. Then Jessica flicked her hair dramatically over her shoulder like something out of a shampoo advert, and shot a look at Josh that said, "Help me!"

Josh sighed. *She's bailed me out hundreds of times*, he thought. *I suppose I can't abandon her now.*

He sucked in a deep breath and then threw his head forward and went into a spectacular coughing fit, clutching the seat in front of him with one hand and mashing the *Call Attendant* button with the other. He opened one watering eye and peered between the seats to see the attendant bow apologetically to Jessica and hurry towards him. Jessica gave him a thumbs up and slipped away into first class.

By the time the attendant had kneeled beside him, patted his back, made sure he wasn't choking, offered to find a doctor, brought him water and insisted on fluffing his complimentary pillow, he felt quite guilty for tricking her. But then, the fake coughing fit made him feel a little sick, so he really was glad of the water.

After the attendant had gone and the bright spots had stopped flashing in front of his eyes, Josh let out a long sigh and slumped in his seat.

Willing Jessica to get to Kiki and back without causing any more trouble, Josh took his sketchpad and pencils out of his bag. He drew a quick sketch of a green bulging monster in a black suit with sunglasses growling into a mobile phone, then one of a cute manga-style Kiki making stupid kissy faces at a small fluffy cloud. He wrote the kanji for "love" over her head. Thanks to Granny Murata insisting on lessons whenever they would visit, Josh knew a few basic kanji. It wasn't enough to be able to read manga in the original language yet, and he was hoping that they might get to learn from more exciting books on this trip. Who needed to know how to write "to whom it may concern" when they could be learning "robot weapons activated" instead?

A shadow fell across him and he looked up.

It was the black-suited hulk.

He loomed over Josh. One enormous hand reached for his pen. Josh moved without really meaning to, one arm coming up to block the bodyguard's hand and the other drawing back, ready to throw a punch. Then he realized what he was doing. The man could probably kill him with his little toe, and he looked like he wanted to. But the bodyguard just snorted and stepped back.

"Josh Murata," he grumbled. "Come now."

Josh had a very bad feeling about this, but there didn't seem to be any alternative. He squeezed out of his seat still clutching his sketchbook and pen, his legs feeling like lead weights. What had Jessica *done*?

Chapter Two

The bodyguard nudged Josh in front of him towards the first-class cabin.

The curtain parted to reveal big plushy seats that reclined all the way down, with little tables next to them, discreet reading lamps and thick, woollen blankets. If he was going to be forced to stay here for the whole flight, Josh decided it might not be so bad. But then the bodyguard shoved him forwards.

Josh looked around for his sister. To his surprise he

heard two female voices giggling, and spotted Jessica sitting beside Kiki, scribbling in her notebook.

"Josh!" Jessica waved him over. "Come and meet Kiki!"

Kiki turned her 100-megawatt smile on Josh. "Hi," she said. Josh felt a grin spread across his face. Jessica had got away with it.

As he walked down the aisle, he saw that the occupied seats were full of snoring, well-dressed business people wearing cashmere eye masks as they slept. The bodyguard loitered in the doorway. Josh was sure he could feel the bodyguard's glare burning into the back of his head like a laser weapon.

He thought hard and finally dragged the right Japanese phrase out of a dusty drawer in his brain.

"*Hajimemashite*," he said, hoping he'd pronounced it right.

Kiki grinned. "I am pleased to meet you, too," she said. "Jessica told me you're an artist."

"Well, I draw a bit," Josh said, holding the sketchbook even tighter.

"Kiki wants you to draw a manga portrait of her for my article," Jessica said.

"Much cooler than a boring photo," Kiki explained.

"Sure!" Josh kneeled in the empty seat in front of Kiki and set his sketchbook on the headrest. He had a good angle on Kiki, but when he looked up he found himself on eye level with the bodyguard, too. An attendant swept up to them and bowed deeply to Kiki.

"Is there anything else I can get for you, miss?" she asked. "We have a wide selection of sodas and teas available."

"Would you two like anything?" Kiki asked.

"Um – a lemonade, thanks!" Jessica grinned. Josh asked for the same, and Kiki ordered iced tea. The attendant left and returned barely thirty seconds later with three clinking glasses and a selection of lemon and lime slices in a tiny porcelain bowl.

"So, what's your favourite type of movie?" Jessica asked, starting a new page in her notebook.

"I like samurai epics," Kiki said, making sweeping arm gestures as if she was wielding a sword. Josh stopped sketching for a moment to make a note to himself on another page – *draw Kiki as samurai later*. "The kind with beautiful women in fantastic gowns battling it out with katanas."

She swept her arm round again and cried, *"Hai!"* Josh saw the bodyguard jump, before he realized Kiki was only playing. One of the passengers lifted her eye mask and glared at them, then turned over, muttering in Japanese.

"Your English is fantastic," Jessica said.

"Arigatō, Jessica," said Kiki, bowing in her seat. "I've enjoyed very much recording songs in English. I hope people like them. Many things Western are really big in Tokyo."

"We're staying with our granny," said Jessica. "She's very traditional, and she doesn't like Western things much."

"Oh, that's a shame," said Kiki. "I love Hollywood and all the famous stars. I like to visit the Tokyo Tower *Ro Ningyokan*." Josh pulled an uncertain face at the Japanese phrase. "The waxworks museum," Kiki said with a smile. "They have lots of new statues this summer. Including a fabulous new one of me!" She smiled with one corner of her mouth quirked up. Josh sketched it in quickly. Yes, that was the expression he wanted, cool and happy. "You'll have to go and see it and tell me what you think."

"What are your plans for the future, after the new album?" Jessica asked.

"Hmm." Kiki shifted in her seat, glancing around at the other passengers. Only a few of them were awake, and they were buried in thick Japanese newspapers or watching an in-flight movie. "You won't publish this for a few weeks, right?" she asked Jessica.

"Right, it's for my school paper," said Jessica. "It'll go out after the summer."

"Well, I have a big secret." Kiki leaned in to Jessica, and Josh bent his head closer to hear. "Every famous girl in Japan auditioned to present *Banzai Banzai Benzaiten*, a brand-new live music show, and I won the job! But nobody knows it's me yet. It's going to be a big surprise."

"Wow!" said Jessica, writing this down. "That's amazing. I can't wait to see it."

"I'm so excited," whispered Kiki. "I get to present the show dressed as Benzaiten, the goddess of water and music. My costume is incredible." Josh made another note – *draw Kiki as Benzaiten: mandolin, river, etc.*

"I think I've finished," he said. He looked down at his sketch. It was pretty good, he thought, as he handed it to Kiki. He watched anxiously as she held up her portrait and studied it. Then she gave Josh another dazzling smile.

"It's fantastic!" she said. "It's just like me. You really are talented. I would love to have a copy."

"I'll make you one," said Josh. "I could do it in colour." He tried his best not to blush.

"Here," Kiki said, borrowing Jessica's pen. She turned over the portrait and wrote something on the back. Josh realized it was an address. He felt a grin spread across his face. Jessica was looking at him with wide, gleeful eyes. "I've liked hanging out with you – why don't you bring the copy round to my apartment? I'll take you to see the *Ro Ningyokan*! Just tell security you're there to see Minnie Mouse, and they'll know I invited you."

"Wow!" Jessica said, her voice going squeaky with excitement. "Cool!" Kiki gave her a hug and shook Josh's hand, and then the bodyguard was suddenly at their side, ushering them back to their seats.

They passed the flight attendant, who did a

spectacular double take to see Jessica going back to her standard class seat. Jessica smiled sweetly, and Josh bowed low, sorry to have tricked her earlier. He clutched his sketchpad, and Jessica kept reading through her notes.

"I don't believe it," she whispered. "Kiki invited us over to her apartment!"

"We've already talked our way in to speak to a pop idol and we're not even out of Europe yet," Josh said, looking out of the window and seeing green, damp-looking fields below. "This could be the best trip ever."

Granny Murata was waiting for them at the Arrivals Gate. She looked serious. As always, she was dressed traditionally, in a lilac kimono printed with climbing vines and little white flowers, tied with a wide silk sash. Her thin arms were folded neatly in front of her.

"Hi, Granny," said Jessica, as they wheeled their suitcases over to her.

One of Granny's eyebrows twitched. *"Ohayō gozaimasu,* Josh-kun, Jessica-chan," she said in formal Japanese.

"*Ohayō*, Granny," Josh replied. Granny gave him a piercing stare. "I mean, *obaasan*," he added quickly. Granny Murata nodded curtly.

"I received an e-mail from your parents. They have arrived safely in Africa. They bring much honour on our family with their work there."

"We're very proud, *obaasan*," Jessica said, with a little bow. Granny nodded again.

"*Tsuitekite*," she commanded. Jessica picked up her suitcase immediately, but it took Josh another second to realize that she'd told them to follow her. As Granny turned to lead them to the car park, he sighed. She was going to want them to talk in Japanese all summer. On the walk through the airport to Granny's battered old Toyota, Josh tried to read the signs written in complicated kanji, but they looked more like intricate spider webs than words.

The Toyota juddered into life and Granny Murata started to pull out of the parking spot. Suddenly Josh and Jessica were thrown forward in their seats as Granny slammed on the brakes and the car creaked to a halt. Josh looked up to find a bright yellow electric hybrid car swerving to avoid their front bumper.

He recognized the driver with a jolt – it was the bodyguard again.

He shot Granny a filthy look as he drove past, and Josh wished someone would put him in his place. Jessica elbowed Josh, and pointed. One of the tinted windows was rolled down and they could see Kiki in the back seat. The twins waved. Kiki spotted them and waved back.

"Hasty young people," Granny Murata said. "They will be the ruin of Japan."

She continued to mutter under her breath as the Toyota pulled away from the airport car park.

Soon Josh found himself looking out at the Tokyo skyline, and knew he was going to have a great summer, even if he did have to sit through some tea ceremony lessons. Tokyo was so cool – the mad combination of skyscrapers and ancient Japanese architecture was like living on another planet. The car pulled up to an intersection where a man in a smart black uniform with pristine white gloves was standing in the middle of the traffic directing cars. Josh grinned as they passed the man and drove on towards Minato Ward. He spotted a skyscraper he'd seen being destroyed by demons in a manga last week. Maybe if Godzilla stomped Granny's house before they got there...

"Hey, look." Jessica pointed out of the window. A billboard up ahead showed a poster advertising *Banzai Banzai Benzaiten* – on both sides were Japanese cheering girls waving red and blue fans, and in the middle was a silhouette of a girl and a question mark above her head. Josh and Jessica grinned at each other.

"Pffft," said Granny Murata. "Modern music turns children into hooligans." Josh tried to imagine Kiki's happy pop music turning anyone into a hooligan. Maybe they would daub graffiti hearts and flowers all over the walls?

They passed the Imperial Palace, with people jogging along the paths, and soon Granny's apartment building loomed into view. Josh let out a sigh. The Sakura Apartments were "a haven of peace and tranquillity" where elderly ladies and gentlemen could live in total uninterrupted boredom. The security system scanned the car as they waited to be admitted to the car park. *Probably checking for people trying to smuggle fun into the building,* Josh thought. After the sensors had turned away from the car, Granny drove up to a bleeping screen. He had been through this several times now but he never quite got used to the way his and Jessica's faces appeared on the screen, or the polite Japanese voice that asked Granny to confirm they were her guests.

As they climbed out of the old Toyota, Granny bowed to another old lady who was shuffling past them towards the elevator. She looked like a walking mummy to Josh – her hands were wrapped in bandages, and she wore a slightly overlarge blue kimono.

"*Ohayō gozaimasu*, Sachiko-san," Granny said. The old lady called Sachiko turned and bowed back.

"*Ohayō*, Murata-san," she said. "These are your English grandchildren?"

"*Hai*." Granny turned to the twins. "Josh-kun, Jessica-chan, this is Sachiko-san."

"*Hajimemashite*, Sachiko-san," Josh and Jessica chorused, bowing. Sachiko beamed at them, showing off a single tooth.

"How sweet," she told Granny. Granny made a "hmph" noise, not exactly a yes or a no.

They followed Sachiko into the lift with their bags and began to rise up through the building towards Granny's apartment on the third floor. Another set of lasers scanned the lift as they reached the second floor. Josh wondered what treasures these elderly people were keeping in their apartments, to need this sort of security. Maybe one of Granny's neighbours was a billionaire.

As they entered Granny's apartment, Josh, Jessica and Granny all stopped on the special rug to swap their shoes for soft white slippers. Josh was surprised that his slippers were new, and they fitted perfectly. Granny must have asked his parents what his shoe size was. Typical Granny – he would have happily walked around in his socks, but she thought of everything.

"I shall prepare your lunch," said Granny. "You can go to your rooms and unpack your things."

"*Dōmō arigatō, obaasan*," said Jessica.

As Granny bowed to Jessica, Josh thought he caught a glimpse of her stony face cracking into a smile.

Granny's apartment was large and mostly empty, decorated in traditional Japanese style with clean lines and simple colours, and no clutter anywhere.

The whole apartment was pretty much the opposite of his room at home, which usually looked like a comic book and a samurai movie had had a fight to the death and nobody had cleaned up afterwards.

Several visits ago, Jessica had claimed the corner room with the big window and the ancient cedarwood *tansu* chest as hers, so Josh made himself comfortable in the other room, dropping his bag onto the end of the neat futon and kicking off his slippers. There was a giant bookshelf all along one wall of the room, and a desk with an antique lamp sitting on it.

Josh reached into his bag and dug around until he found the little padded case that carried his portable games console and its discs. He hoped he'd be able to get some serious gaming in this summer. He flicked the switch and the console screen lit up, then gave a sad little *woop* and went dark again. *The battery must be dead*. Josh looked at his charger, with its three rectangular pins, then back at the Japanese socket with its two rounded holes. He sighed. He knew exactly where his converter was. It was sitting on his bedside table, in London. Groaning, Josh put the console back in its case.

If he didn't have his video games, he was going to have to find something else to occupy his time until Granny's lessons began. He wandered up to the bookshelf that he'd never paid much attention to before and looked at the spines of the books. He'd expected them all to be written in kanji, but now that he looked at them some were actually in English and looked really cool. He spotted a big leather bound book called *A History of the Samurai* and opened it. The front page was taken up with a huge, intricately detailed painting of the samurai warlord Mōri Motonari and his pirate allies sailing to the island of Miyajima.

Josh left the book on the desk and looked at some of the others. To his surprise, there were plenty of interesting books hidden amongst the etiquette and gardening manuals. He laid some out on the floor so he could look at them all together. Then he spotted another book that looked much older than the rest. Its spine was made of red leather with intricate gold and silver vines worked into its surface. The title was in kanji, but he recognized the words "Ninja" and "Secrets" from a manga he'd tried to translate once.

Now that's a book worth reading! He prised it out from between two thick tomes on tax collection in the Edo period – and then something caught his eye.

Instead of a blank wall behind the book, he found himself looking at a small blinking red light. That was weird. Could it be a fire alarm, or some kind of electrical safety switch? Why would it be hidden behind the books? Puzzled, he lifted down one of the tax collection books, and spotted a small metal panel set into the wall. Except it wasn't actually the wall – the whole back of the bookcase seemed to be made of metal.

"That *is* weird," he muttered. He pulled some more books off the shelves, until he could see the whole panel. It had the blinking red light on one side, a darkened green bulb on the other, and a keypad in the middle with numbers on it, both in kanji and English. Josh blinked at it for a second, in case he was hallucinating. But no, he wasn't imagining things. It was clearly and without doubt the keypad to open some kind of secret safe.

"Hey," said a voice. "Whatcha doing?"

"Nothing!" Josh squealed, whirling round and doing

his best to cover the empty bookshelves with his outstretched arms.

Jessica gave him a suspicious look. "What did you break?" Josh let out a sigh of relief. He could tell Jess would get the truth out of him somehow.

"Nothing, really," Josh protested. "Look."

Jessica peered into the bookshelf. "Huh," she said.

"Is that all you can say? It's a secret safe!"

"Josh, you saw the laser scanners and the guards on the lobby, right?" Jessica shrugged. "This place is full of security tech. It's a luxury retirement home for the extremely paranoid."

"But what would Granny keep in a safe like this? You're not curious?"

"Come on, Josh," Jessica rolled her eyes. "This is Granny Murata we're talking about. She only figured out e-mail a few months ago. She probably doesn't use it." Josh looked back at the safe. "I'm going to see if lunch is ready," Jessica said. "Cool books, though."

Maybe Jessica was right about the safe, but Josh didn't think so. He felt as though he'd walked straight into the pages of a comic book. There could be *anything* in that safe. And why *did* Granny live here anyway, if not for security? *Something is definitely in there*, Josh thought, looking back at the safe. *And I'm going to find out what.*

Chapter Three

"Have you finished unpacking?"

Granny Murata! Josh turned to find Granny standing in his doorway.

"Umm…" Josh hesitated, then kicked himself for looking so guilty. He hadn't heard Granny arrive – in those soft indoor shoes she could move like a ninja. "Yes," he said, "I've finished." *Oh, lying to Granny*, he thought to himself. *Very smooth*.

"Good," Granny said. "I would like you to visit a

friend of mine before lunch." Josh froze. That didn't sound good. "Mr. Yamamoto is eighty-five years old, mostly confined to his bed, and his children do not come to see him often – he would enjoy a visit from a young man such as yourself."

Josh contemplated an afternoon spent with a bedridden eighty-five-year-old Japanese stranger, and wondered if it was too late to jump in the Pacific Ocean and swim back to England.

Mr. Yamamoto's apartment was on the floor below Granny Murata's. Josh knocked softly, half hoping the old man might be asleep. But he clearly heard a voice call out "Come in!" and found that the door wasn't locked.

"No luck," Josh muttered as he stepped inside.

The layout of the apartment was much like Granny Murata's, but there were a lot more things in it – the sitting room was crowded with cabinets filled with ornaments and random objects, and two big tables piled with papers and odd electrical gadgets. Josh slid his shoes off.

He peered into what he guessed might be a bedroom. He was right – all around the walls there were more cluttered cabinets, and in the middle of the room was a large bed with a small bald man lying in it, blinking happily at him.

"Josh-kun, am I right?" he asked.

"Yes," Josh said. "*Konnichiwa*, Yamamoto-san," he added, bowing.

"Come here, let me see you," said Mr. Yamamoto, raising one bony hand and beckoning him over. "My eyes are not what they used to be. Sit, sit." He gestured to a seat beside the bed.

Close up, Mr. Yamamoto was tanned and extremely wrinkled, like a piece of old leather that had been stretched, left out in the rain and then dried out again. He smelled of old stale tobacco.

"My second wife was English, you know." Mr. Yamamoto smiled broadly, revealing a set of slightly overlarge false teeth. "Fine woman. You know what she did for a living?" Josh opened his mouth, but the old man ploughed straight on, a dreamy look coming over his face. "She was a ballerina. When she retired she ran children's parties. Or..." His face crinkled up with thought. "…was that Josette? My third wife. She was French, very tall, made the most amazing *bento*… not as beautiful as Haruhi."

Josh realized Mr. Yamamoto was looking at him expectantly. His attention had wandered. He had been gazing out of the window over the Tokyo skyline, imagining superheroes swinging between the buildings, fighting to bring down a giant robot army.

He dragged his brain back to the conversation.

"Haruhi," he said. "Was that your first wife?"

"*Fourth*," said Mr. Yamamoto, grinning broadly. "Now she really was special… Do something for me, Josh-kun," he said. "Pass me a spoonful of that rice." Josh picked up the bowl of rice that sat on the table beside Mr. Yamamoto's bed, and scooped up some of the rice using its wide china spoon. He was about to try to pass the spoon to the old man, when he realized Mr. Yamamoto wasn't moving to take it. "My hands shake," he said, lifting his chin expectantly.

Josh gingerly raised the spoon to Mr. Yamamoto's wrinkled lips. The old man leaned forwards and wrapped his lips around the spoon. But then Josh didn't know what to do – should he wait for the old man to swallow, or should he try to pull the spoon away, or what? He went for pulling away. It was the wrong thing to do. A thin line of rice and dribble splatted onto Mr. Yamamoto's front.

"Oh, sorry!" Josh grimaced, grabbing a tissue from a box beside the rice bowl and trying to wipe the rice away without making it worse. "*Sumimasen*, Yamamoto-san!" But to Josh's relief, Mr. Yamamoto didn't look angry – he laughed.

"That's all right, Josh-kun. Let's leave the rice for now. Where was I? Oh, Josette. She was a beauty. She made flowers..." Mr. Yamamoto yawned. "...out of silk, and...she was a pilot...or was that Chiyoko? Dear Chiyoko...always smelled of...engine oil..."

Josh waited for the rest of the sentence, but it never came. Mr. Yamamoto's head fell back on the pillow and he was soon snoring like a motorbike revving up in a wind tunnel.

Once again, Josh found himself looking for something to do. There were lots of very old books on the shelves, ancient things with fabric flaking off their spines. But unlike Granny Murata's nice neat bookshelves, these were stacked in messy, teetering piles, and in between them there was a forest of... *stuff*. It looked like junk to Josh. There were scraps of paper, tiny porcelain models of birds and fish, a bunch of silk flowers that Josh guessed were made by Josette – or was it Haruhi? – a sadly tattered collection of old ribbons, a pair of gleaming kama...

...*Kama*? Josh blinked and rubbed his eyes, but there they were – two silvery weapons, like the miniature scythes that farmers used to harvest crops, half-hidden under an old porcelain dragon with several fangs missing. They looked clean and razor-sharp, as if they'd been polished yesterday. Josh glanced back at Mr. Yamamoto. He was still snoring and now drooling slightly.

Maybe they're not really as sharp as they look, Josh thought. But then his eyes strayed over to another cabinet, and there was a pair of nunchaku with bright silver swans painted on their sides. Now that he was looking, he could spot sai daggers sticking out of a vase, and polished wooden tonfa being used to prop up a wobbly shelf. He peered closer and reached up to open the cabinet. He'd never seen these things outside movies and manga – what were they doing in the apartment of a little old man, hidden under a load of strange old junk?

"What..." Mr. Yamamoto spluttered. Josh jumped, and tried to look like he hadn't been snooping. The old man sighed and continued as if he hadn't fallen asleep. "Oh yes, the smell of engine oil – that's what I remember. Good old Chiyoko." The old man went on, and Josh sidled back across the room and sat down in the chair again. He was such a feeble-looking wrinkled old man, but he had such awesome weapons in his collection. Josh wondered if there was a story in that – he could write a comic about an elderly man who used to be a fighter, battling black-clad villains with whirling nunchaku in each hand, rescuing his five glamorous wives from evil Yakuza bosses. It'd make a pretty awesome comic, Josh decided.

Finally, Mr. Yamamoto's monologue rolled to a halt and he thanked Josh for visiting. Josh took the elevator back upstairs, still mentally laying out fight scenes from the comic, which he'd decided to call *Mr. Y's Golden Years*. He made a beeline for his bedroom and threw a quick sad glance at his games console with its Japanese two-pronged plug—

Wait. Its *Japanese* plug? He looked again. He blinked hard and rubbed his eyes and then looked *again*. It was definitely there, neatly wired into the charger, a plug of exactly the right sort to fit into Granny's power sockets.

He poked his head into Jessica's room, where she was scribbling in a notebook and chewing on her pen lid.

"Hey Jess, did you bring my Japanese console plug?"

She looked up at him and shrugged.

"Nope," she said.

"It's just – I could have sworn—"

"You forgot it?" Jessica asked, pulling a sympathetic face.

"Yes, I mean, I thought I had. But now it's right there, wired in and everything."

"You must've just missed it before," she said. "Only rational explanation. Oh, unless – I know," she said, with a totally deadpan expression, "Granny must have sneaked in and rewired it for you."

"Oh right. Yes, that must be it." They looked at each other for a few seconds. But Josh couldn't keep it up for long – he could feel the laugh start at the bottom of his chest and work its way up through his throat. He cracked up.

"Ha!" Jessica crowed. "I win! I am the Queen of the Straight Face Game."

"You always win." Josh bowed to her, still sniggering. "Granny rewired the plug! She wouldn't know a fuse from a hairpin." He went back into his room, shooting another glance at the games console and then putting it out of his mind.

"Come and have your lunch," Granny said, appearing in the doorway a few minutes later. Josh followed her beckoning, bony finger into the dining room. It was as clean and traditionally decorated as the rest of the apartment, with a few concessions to the modern age – as well as the low wooden table surrounded by cushioned seats, there was a worktop containing a pair of silver steamers and a sparkling hotplate.

Jessica was already sitting at the table, gazing at the food Granny Murata had laid out for them. Josh felt his mouth start to water at the sight of the little bowls of rice, slivers of fresh ginger, sliced tuna, and pork dumplings wrapped in dough with spicy sauce to dip them in. He quickly slid into a seat and waited for Granny to make herself comfortable.

"*Itadakimasu*," Jessica said.

Josh nodded fervently. "Yeah, thanks!" he grinned.

Granny nodded solemnly to them both and picked up her chopsticks. Josh dug into the dumplings and rice balls.

When the meal was nearly over, Granny's phone chirped. She apologized and excused herself to the kitchen to answer it.

"Granny's cooking is the best," Josh said, slurping down the last of his broth.

"Agreed," Jessica replied, setting her chopsticks down on their holder.

Granny returned and collected their empty bowls. "Josh, Jessica. Will you two go to the mall for me now? I need some groceries for dinner tonight but I am feeling tired."

"Sure!" Josh said, happy to go exploring in the city.

"Here is my list," Granny said. She handed over a piece of paper. It was all written in kanji.

Josh felt his face heat up. He was rubbish at the

Straight Face Game. "Hm," said Granny Murata. "You see how useful it is to know your kanji. Take this also." She handed over a second piece of paper, this time with the list written down twice – once in transliterated Japanese and once in English. "Use this to learn," she said.

"*Hai*," Josh and Jessica chorused.

Granny Murata had sent them off to the mall with a wallet full of yen and a mobile phone in case they got lost. But as soon as Josh walked up to the huge glass front doors, he was sure that getting lost was inevitable. The mall towered over them and sprawled out, all brightly coloured bricks and giant windows. In the massive entrance lobby there was a map showing six floors and eighteen separate shopping districts, with tiny kanji lettering and arrows. Jessica pointed suddenly.

"There!" she said. "That's the grocery store. See, the kanji matches this one on Granny's list." They set off, passing noodle stalls decorated with beads; gangs of teenaged girls in identical outfits with exactly the same stripy socks, short pink skirts and pink goggles on top of their heads; giant light displays advertising soft drinks and candy; and gleaming white shopfronts that didn't seem to be selling anything at all.

They passed an electronics shop decked out in sparkling lights. Josh stopped in his tracks when he saw the window display.

"It's the new Starplayer," he breathed, gazing at the sleek white machine. "It's the new generation of video games – backwards and sideways compatibility, 200 gig of memory, touch screen and laser sensor interface, and full exclusive rights to the Star Knight franchise – and it's not going to be sold in Europe for the next *five years*."

"And even then there's no way you'll be able to afford one," said Jessica wistfully.

She wandered off to look at the other cool gadgets in the window, leaving Josh to sigh at the Starplayer. The power of its awesomeness sucked him in until there seemed to be nothing else in the world but him and its shiny buttons.

"Hey, Josh. Look at this!" Jessica said, bringing him back down to earth with a poke in the shoulder blades. "It's Kiki. I think she's on the news." Josh turned to look. In another window of the electronics shop, a collection of massive High Definition TV screens showed a serious-looking newsreader in a pink suit beside a photo of Kiki. "Look, I found one with English...subtitles..." Jessica began, but trailed off as she read the translation of the kanji that was scrolling along the bottom of the screens.

Bodyguard sustains several injuries. Authorities call for any witnesses to go to the police. Chiba Mikiko abducted in Tokyo.

"Josh," Jessica gasped. "Kiki's been kidnapped!"

Chapter Four

Jessica rushed inside the shop and Josh followed. Now they could hear the newsreader's voice – the shop manager had turned the volume up and most of the customers were staring in disbelief at the TV screens.

"In dramatic scenes in Minato Ward earlier today," the newsreader's subtitle read, "Chiba Mikiko's loyal bodyguard stumbled into a police box, with several injuries to his face and arms, and told officers that a masked thug broke into Chiba-san's car and abducted the popular singer as they travelled from Tokyo Airport to her penthouse apartment."

Josh and Jessica stared at each other. Josh thought of the friendly girl on the aeroplane and blinked hard – this couldn't be happening! Jessica was wide-eyed and clutching her shopping bag so hard her knuckles had turned white.

"What can we do?" she asked. "Maybe we were the last to see her! Maybe we should talk to the police?"

The newsreader cut to a live report of Kiki's bodyguard making a speech outside her apartment building. Josh stared as the hulking, suited man appeared at the top of a flight of concrete steps. He had a black eye and a large purple bruise spreading across his jaw.

As he watched, Josh got the feeling that he knew those steps. In fact, the whole scene, the gleaming glass doors and polished silver railings of the building, was ringing a huge, loud bell in Josh's head.

"I know that place!" he said. "That's just round the corner from here. We could..." He wasn't sure how to finish the sentence – what more could they do there? But Jessica finished it for him.

"Let's go," she said, heading for the door.

As they reached the apartment building, Josh realized they weren't the only ones who'd had the idea of going round to see what was going on. As they turned a corner and the building came into sight, they nearly ran into a group of girls who were walking towards the steps chattering worriedly. A crowd had already gathered outside Kiki's apartment.

"How could they do this?" one of the girls wailed. "Who would want to hurt Kiki?"

Josh and Jessica weaved through a group of teenagers holding up hastily scrawled banners saying *We ♥ you Kiki* and *Give us back our Kiki* and passed two women weeping hysterically on each other's shoulders.

Police barriers surrounded the building's entrance, where the bodyguard was appealing to a row of TV cameras.

"We were prepared to deal with an incident of this

nature," he growled, "but we were taken by surprise on the road. Mikiko-sama was very frightened on the aeroplane," the bodyguard went on. "She had received some upsetting hate mail."

"That's not true!" Jessica said loudly. Josh "sshhed" her, and she frowned at him. "But it's not," she said more quietly. "We were there; she was fine! She said she *liked* her fan mail; I've still got my notes."

"She could have been just...trying to keep her spirits up?" Josh suggested, but he didn't believe it himself. Kiki's publicist, a woman in a bright red suit with hair that stuck straight up from her head, took over from the bodyguard.

"Please," she said, her eyes filling with tears. "Whoever has taken our Kiki – please let her come back!"

Josh watched the bodyguard carefully, as the focus of the crowd's attention slid over to the publicist. The man stalked down from the steps, cracking his knuckles.

"He doesn't look badly injured," he said.

"You ran into him in the airport," Jessica said. "Did he seem like he could be overcome by a single thug in a confined space? Or thrown out of a car he didn't want to be thrown out of?"

"Not in a million years," Josh said. Beside them a young woman groaned sadly at something the publicist had said, and a man put his arm around her.

"He's having a bit of an off day then, isn't he? And how did the kidnappers know exactly where the car would be so they could jump in? And" – Jessica's eyes glinted with the excitement of a journalist onto a hot story – "why weren't the car doors locked in the first place if they were so security conscious?"

Josh didn't have an answer. There was no answer. Except… "It's all lies." Saying it out loud gave Josh shivers down the back of his neck, but there wasn't any other explanation. "Something happened to Kiki, and that bodyguard's lying about it."

"Look, he's answering his phone," Jessica said, pointing to the police barriers where the bodyguard was slipping away with a small black phone clamped to his giant ear.

"I wish I knew what he was saying—" Josh began, but Jessica was already dodging her way through the hysterical crowd. "Jess – wait!" Josh went after her, catching up when she had to find her way through a circle of women holding hands and singing one of Kiki's famous love songs. Together they ducked and weaved until they spotted the bodyguard turning down an alleyway, still talking into his mobile phone. They ran after him.

The alley was dark and dingy, lined with large rubbish bins where the nearby shops dumped their waste. Graffiti was scrawled up the walls, a mixture of kanji and English-style graffiti lettering.

The bodyguard had stopped a little way down. Josh and Jessica crept closer, darting from behind a pile of discarded boxes to leap into a hidden doorway, then racing to kneel beside a large green rubbish bin. They had drawn near enough to hear what the big man was saying.

"Yes, Boss," he said. "I did, Boss."

"*Kiki?*" Josh mouthed. Jessica shook her head.

"*Don't think so,*" she mouthed back.

"Yes, Boss," the bodyguard repeated. "She is on her way." Suddenly he laughed. "Ha! Ha! People are so stupid. They will all see Chiba and not know it! Very clever, Boss." He moved away down the alley.

"He knows where Kiki is!" Jessica hissed. "We have to go after him, maybe he'll lead us to her." Josh nodded. Carefully, the two of them followed, watching where they put their feet in case they trod on something that would make a noise.

"You know, if this was a comic book, we'd be walking right into a trap," he whispered.

"Oh *thanks*," Jessica muttered. "I'm *so* much more relaxed now."

They crept further into the alley, which looked like it was coming to a dead end, stepping over discarded bottles, keeping the bodyguard in sight. A rat scuttled under one of the bins, and Josh suppressed a shudder. Suddenly Jessica poked him in the back.

"Ow – what?" he hissed. Then he turned to see what she'd seen: two more men in black suits coming down the alley after them. Josh looked back and saw that the bodyguard had turned around and was walking towards them. They were surrounded.

"Not good," Josh said through gritted teeth. "Really not good..." The men came closer, and Josh tried to stand up straight and not look like he was sneaking anywhere. He plastered a bright smile on his face.

"Hullo," he began. "Um, my sister and I are lost... *hagu...re...ta*?" he said, making sure to pronounce the Japanese badly.

"Can you gents tell us the way back to the mall?" Jessica joined in. "Our father must be looking for us..."

The men in suits didn't answer.

"We'll be off, then..." Josh said. He grabbed Jessica's hand and launched himself into a run, aiming straight between the two men and the alley entrance. But one of the men shot out a huge arm and pushed him back. Jessica cannoned into him and they both almost fell to the ground.

"Hey—" Josh began, but then a familiar growling voice from behind cut him off.

"Stop them!" it said in Japanese. "I know them – meddling English from the plane." Josh and Jessica turned to find Kiki's bodyguard in front of them. "We take them in," he said. "Until it's all over."

A pair of strong hands came down on Josh's shoulders. Josh wasn't about to let himself be taken anywhere. He seized one of the man's wrists and twisted away, holding on tight and bending the arm around with him. The man let out a surprised yell, before grabbing at Josh's throat with his other hand. Josh ducked away, and saw that Jessica had tried a similar move, but not succeeded – her attacker had an iron grip on both her wrists. She writhed and pulled but couldn't free herself. Then Josh choked as the bodyguard's arm closed around his throat.

He managed to get one good backhand blow in on the bodyguard's nose, and the big man dropped him. He rolled away from the other suited man's boot as it headed for his face and heard a loud, "*Hai!*" A second later he saw Jessica lash out with one foot getting her attacker between the legs with the pointy end of her shoes. The man crumpled to his knees with a yell. Sensei Neil from their dojo would be proud.

"Yeah, go Jess!" Josh cried. He shot to his feet and managed to dodge the bodyguard. Jessica pulled away from the other man, and then they were sprinting away towards hope and freedom and safety…and the brick wall at the wrong end of the alley.

They stopped and turned back. The three men were advancing on them with bared teeth.

"I knew you stupid children would be trouble," growled the bodyguard.

Josh and Jessica both took up their ready stances, like Sensei Neil had taught them, with their weight evenly distributed and one hand up ready to parry a first blow. But Josh's arms were aching and he could hear Jessica breathing fast. It was two against three. Josh tried to push his brain into a higher gear, looking for a way out. But they were trapped.

Suddenly, Josh heard a noise above them. He looked to see something falling out of the sky. The bodyguard and the two men in suits looked up too, frowning in confusion.

"What's that?" Jessica cried.

Josh could see that it was a person, dressed all in black, zipping down from the roof on a wire. About half a second later the figure's feet landed right in the middle of the bodyguard's face. Josh pressed himself back against the wall as the bodyguard fell to his knees.

The mysterious figure used the bodyguard's face like a springboard and leaped into the air. The attacker twisted and landed a kick on each of the other men's necks before somersaulting back to the ground with a graceful flourish.

The black-clad figure raised its hands in challenge to the thugs, who growled and rolled up their sleeves.

"Yay! Go…mysterious ninja!" Jessica cried.

The figure executed a perfect spinning high kick to the first thug's face, sending him reeling. The second thug tried to grab hold but their rescuer used his momentum to bounce the man's head off the wall.

The bodyguard scrambled to his feet, blood streaming from a broken nose, and stumbled away down the alley.

Josh was stunned. This was a superhero. A real life, seriously for serious superhero had just rescued *him*! The person turned, hands on hips.

"Well? *Nigero!*" came the command.

"Okay, we're going!" Jessica said. She grabbed Josh's hand and tried to pull him away. He dug his heels into the concrete – there was no way he was going to be yanked away before he found out who their superhero really was. "Come *on*, Josh, don't upset the dangerous ninja," Jessica said through her teeth.

No way, Josh thought. The hero's hood was coming loose from its top. If he could just reach it...

As Jessica dragged him past, he wrenched his wrist free, reached up and pulled the black fabric hood. It slid off, smooth as silk.

Underneath there was a flash of grey hair, pale skin, serious brown eyes...wrinkles...thin lips pursed in an expression of annoyance. Josh's hero shot out a hand, quicker than the eye could follow and grabbed him by the wrist.

"Josh Murata, you return that to me this instant!" said Granny Murata.

Chapter Five

Josh dropped the hood. Granny scooped it up, brushing the dirt off. She sighed at Josh and Jessica, then her hands shot out and cuffed them both around the head.

"Foolish, foolish children!" she said. "You wander off alone; you follow a suspicious man three times the size of both of you put together; you do this—" She brandished the mask. "Worst of all, you compromise my mission!"

"Your…" Josh croaked.

"Your *mission*?" Jessica asked.

Granny Murata sighed. "You think I do this for my health?" she said. She glanced around, checking for eavesdroppers. "We can't talk about it here." She unzipped her black jacket, took it off and turned it inside out. Josh was amazed to see that the lining was made of light blue silk with a pattern of white flowers. She shrugged the jacket back on, and suddenly she was no longer a secret ninja – she was just an elderly lady, dressed in a modern blue silk jacket over a black vest and black trousers. "Right. Home."

When they got back to the apartment Granny led them straight to Josh's room. He was a bit embarrassed that he'd left books scattered over the floor. Granny stepped neatly over them and approached the bookshelf. If she was surprised to see that he'd already found the secret safe, she didn't show it.

"Move these, please, and stand back," she said, gesturing to the books. Josh and Jessica scrambled to pick up the books. Granny Murata reached over the shelf and tapped out a code on the keypad. Josh saw the red light go out and the green light flicker on, and then there was an enormous *clang* and the whole bookshelf started to swing outwards. Josh and Jessica watched as the secret door revealed an elevator with shiny silver panelling and a set of gleaming multicoloured buttons.

Granny entered the elevator and stood there, eyebrow raised and arms crossed.

"Come along, then," she ordered. Josh hurried in and Jessica followed, hastily dumping the books. The bookcase door swung back and the elevator started to descend.

An illuminated map of the building was etched into a glass panel on one wall. As Josh watched, a floating blue light travelled down the map from Granny's third floor apartment. One floor, two, three...they were beside the lobby now but the elevator kept on falling, down below the basement and the car park level. The light kept moving too, into the unknown blank space under the Sakura Apartments where there was nothing marked on the glass.

"This is amazing, *obaasan*," said Jessica. "Where does it go?"

"You'll see," Granny said. Josh saw her cheek twitch as if she was trying not to smile at some private joke.

The light reached the bottom of the glass panel and the elevator stopped. The door swung open, and in front of them...

"Now that," Josh said, "is *incredible*."

The room looked like it had been designed by a manga artist. Giant screens showed infrared and 3D views of Tokyo buildings, swish black leather chairs were pulled up to glittering control panels, and the far wall was filled with racks of weapons – gleaming katana, polished tonfa and pairs of elaborately painted nunchaku.

A figure was standing in front of the racks. He slotted a sword into its place on the wall, and turned around. It was Mr. Yamamoto. He was standing perfectly straight, looking fit and healthy and definitely not bedridden! His eyes met Josh's, and he grinned. He picked up a long wooden staff and rolled it in his hands before twirling it over his shoulder and around his waist so fast it became a blur. The old man with the junk collection looked like he could do some serious damage!

Josh felt his face go bright red. "I suppose he can probably feed himself his own rice, then," he muttered.

"Ah, Josh-kun," Mr. Yamamoto said, with a theatrical wink at Granny Murata. He finished his display and put the staff back on the rack. "Mimi, a pleasure as always," he said to Granny, bowing low. "But perhaps your age is showing, being unmasked by a child."

Granny rolled her eyes. "Yamamoto-san is my weapons expert," she said, steering Josh and Jessica into the room.

Josh remembered the weapons he found in Mr. Yamamoto's apartment.

"And this is Sachiko-san," Granny said, indicating the grey-haired lady seated in front of a bank of CCTV screens with a massive, complex selection of buttons and slides at her fingertips.

Sachiko-san was the little old lady from the parking garage. She looked different now – she had one arm draped over the back of her chair in a very un-grandmotherly way, and where the bandages had been wrapped around her arms the wrinkled skin was covered in ancient tattoos. She grinned at them with a set of sparkling false teeth.

"Sachiko-san is my disguise technician and an aikido master," said Granny. "Are the others out on a mission, Sachiko?"

"Others?" Josh said, still confused.

"They're sparring next door," said Sachiko, punching a few buttons on the control panel. "I'll ask them to come in – I'm sure they're dying to meet your grandchildren."

"My grandchildren who may have compromised our mission," Granny said.

Josh swallowed hard.

"Sachiko, please show us the footage," Granny ordered.

"*Hai,*" said Sachiko and in an instant, up on three of the screens was a view of the crowd outside Kiki's apartment building.

Jessica nudged Josh in the ribs. "It's us!" she exclaimed. The twins could be seen making their way through the people, the moment where they started following the bodyguard towards the alley.

"Imagine my surprise," Granny said. "My team was in the middle of a criminal surveillance mission when they spotted my grandchildren – not at the shopping mall buying vegetables."

"Um," Josh didn't know what to say.

A door on the opposite wall slid open. Three more elderly people entered the room through a door to their left, wearing black martial arts uniforms and each carrying a katana – long, curved Japanese swords.

"Ah – here are the members of my team you have not yet met. This is Nana-san, Mimasu-san and Nakamura-san."

"Nana-san is my head of surveillance," Granny said. "She is able to tap into any CCTV camera in the city." The tall lady in the centre of the group bowed to Josh and Jessica and then slid into the seat next to Sachiko. Nana seemed a bit younger than the others, though she still couldn't have been less than sixty-five.

"Nakamura-san is my medical expert," Granny continued. Nakamura was the shortest and looked like he must be at least a hundred years old. He nodded smartly to the twins.

"And finally, Mimasu-san is our technology expert."

Sachiko grinned widely. "In her civilian life, she is a master chef."

"She once killed twelve men with an electrified spatula," Mr. Yamamoto whispered, leaning close to Josh's ear.

"Er... *ha-hajimemashite*," Josh stammered. Jessica bowed clumsily.

"*Hajimemashite*, kids," said Sachiko, with a nod.

"Granny – what *is* this?" Jessica asked.

"I wish I did not have to show you any of this, but I had no choice once you found out who I was. This is Team Obaasan," she told them. "Team O is an elite, undercover, intelligence-gathering and crime-fighting unit of the National Police, operating under the Japanese Government."

Ninja spies! Josh could tell from Granny's tone that this was very serious, and that he should try to treat it seriously and not as the *most awesome thing he'd ever seen*. He caught Jessica's eye and nearly cracked up – she was trying not to grin, too.

"The Sakura Apartment complex is our cover," Granny continued. "Nobody will ever suspect a group of elderly people of doing the work we do."

You can say that again, Josh thought.

"What a secret!" Jessica said. "Just think, all those times we came to visit you…"

"I never would have guessed," Josh put in.

"It has been difficult sometimes," Granny replied. "But I must stay undercover at all costs. Team O has many enemies who would bring us down. While we may be older than your average crime fighter, I have found the most skilled, most disciplined, most loyal crew imaginable." Josh saw each member of the group give Granny a small, grateful nod. "Today, our job is to find Chiba Mikiko," Granny finished.

Jessica stared. "You know about Kiki?" she asked. "And the kidnapping?"

"Of course. I have all her albums," said Granny. "During lunch, I received a call from HQ to say she had been kidnapped – that was why I asked you to go out. I *thought* I might be able to keep you out of trouble," she added pointedly.

"Um. Sorry, Granny," said Jessica. "But we had to follow that security guard."

"Yeah, we knew that bodyguard was lying when he said Kiki was scared by her fan mail," Josh put in.

"How do you know this?" Granny asked. All of Team O was watching the twins.

Jessica took a deep breath. "We talked to Kiki on the plane and she was really happy. The only one who was acting weird was the bodyguard."

Josh remembered him talking furiously on his mobile before the flight. "He must have been planning this for ages."

The old people exchanged glances and Granny grunted.

"We think that Kiki has been taken by the Iron Fist wing of the Yakuza," said Nana, punching a few buttons on her console. Photographs of the criminal gang flashed up on the screens in front of them – several pictures of large men in dark suits, and blurry shots of fighters wielding swords. In the middle there was a photo of an elderly man with a gaunt face and long grey hair tied up in a ponytail, grinning at the camera, a single gold tooth glinting. "That is Mr. Yoshida. The leader of the Iron Fist."

"But what would the Yakuza want with Kiki?" Josh asked.

"Is it money?" Jessica suggested. "They haven't

asked for a ransom yet."

"Well-noticed, Jessica," Nana said. "We don't think it's anything to do with Kiki's millions. You might be surprised to hear that she is not the first pop idol to be targeted."

"Really?" Josh asked. "But if other pop stars have gone missing, wouldn't we have heard about it?"

"Ah, but they haven't been going missing," said Mr. Yamamoto. "Nana, if you would?" Nana pressed more buttons. Around the central photo of Mr. Yoshida, the faces of the Yakuza were replaced by a handful of Japanese pop stars who Josh vaguely recognized.

Nana pointed to each one in turn. "Saika Oshiro's recording sessions for her new album have been plagued by power cuts and technical failure. A computer error left thousands of Tokyo Ono's fans with invalid tickets for their tour. Takeo Kimura even had all his hair shaved off in the night!" Jessica gasped.

"We've traced all these 'accidents' to the Iron Fist," said Granny. "Yamamoto-san scanned the scenes of the incidents and found fingerprints belonging to Mr. Yoshida's minions. Now, it seems, they have taken their pop idol persecution a step further."

"But why? What has this Mr. Yoshida got against pop singers?" Jessica asked.

"Unfortunately," Granny admitted, "we don't know that yet." She stared at the picture of Mr. Yoshida and narrowed her eyes. "Nana, play our profile of Mr. Yoshida." Nana punched another button and a robotic voice began to speak over a slide show of photos of the Yakuza boss.

"Yoshida Noboru, seventy-eight. Boss of the Iron Fist Yakuza group. To the outside world, he is a respectable businessman, owning chains of restaurants, karaoke bars, hotels, golf resorts, museums and tourist attractions. In reality, the Iron Fist has been linked to smuggling, high profile theft, espionage, blackmail and murder. He is divorced, and has one granddaughter."

"Thanks to you two and your alleyway incident, we know that Kiki's bodyguard was in league with the Iron Fist," said Sachiko. "He must have handed her over and faked injuries to make it look like she was kidnapped – but after that, we don't know where she was taken to."

"We do know something," Jessica said. Team O all

turned to her. She looked at Josh, and he nodded.

"We overheard the bodyguard on the phone – he was calling someone boss, so maybe he was talking to Mr. Yoshida."

"He said Kiki was somewhere where everyone could see her, but no one would know it was her."

"Very interesting!" Nana said, typing something into a keyboard near her right hand.

"So," Jessica continued, "I was thinking, she could be on top of a building somewhere, or maybe she's been put in disguise, or they're hiding her in a Kiki tribute band…"

"We could help—" Josh began.

But Granny put a hand on his shoulder. "That's enough, both of you. I have shown you our operation because it will be easier for us all if you are aware of my work. Clearly, I cannot rely on you to keep yourselves out of trouble. But you are not to get involved with this investigation."

"But Granny, we *can* help! I'm sure we can!" Jessica protested. Granny shook her head.

"As soon as you became involved with Team O, you became a target. I cannot risk your safety. Think of what your parents would say if you were hurt." Their parents... Josh frowned suddenly, his mind flooding with questions that he'd been too stunned to think of until now – how long had Granny Murata been a secret ninja agent? Had she ever actually been a schoolteacher, like their dad had told them? And most importantly...

"*Obaasan*, our parents!" Josh exclaimed. "Do they know about this?"

"No, Josh. And you can never tell them. They are far happier and safer if they do not know. Now, we really must go back upstairs. The jet lag must be about to catch up with you both. You need to get straight to bed."

The rest of Team O waved them off, and they got back into the lift. Josh traced the light up and up across the glass display until it reached the third floor, and then the door swung open and they were back in his room, with the desk scattered with books and pencils.

"Now, straight to bed," said Granny. Josh didn't feel tired. He felt like he could take on the world – with the help of his granny's superhero ninja team, of course.

"G'night Josh," Jessica said. "See you tomorrow." She raised an eyebrow at him and Josh nodded back.

Who knows what we'll see tomorrow? thought Josh.

"Night," Josh replied. Granny ushered Jessica into the hall, and closed the door behind her.

Josh settled down on his futon and pulled his sketchbook out of his bag. He sat still for a second, composing his thoughts, and then he started drawing storyboards, mapping out an idea for a great new comic character.

My Ninja Granny...

Chapter Six

"Josh, wake up!"

He opened his eyes. Granny was standing beside his bed, wearing her sleek black ninja outfit. Josh sat up so fast his head spun. "You have thirty seconds to get dressed," Granny said, tapping the black and white sheath of a small katana against her leg. Josh tumbled out of bed, fumbling for his T-shirt. Granny nodded curtly and left the room.

Twenty-seven and a half seconds later, Josh hopped

out of his room still pulling on his socks and nearly collided with Jessica, who was stumbling into the corridor, trying to dislodge a brush that was tangled in her hair. Granny was standing at the door, arms folded, back as straight as a steel rod. A sword hung from her belt.

"Good," she said. "*Tsuitekite*." She marched out of the apartment, stepping into her outdoor shoes and through the door in one smooth motion. Josh and Jessica scrambled to keep up with her.

Once in the lift, Granny held up one finger for their attention.

"Watch me; you may need to remember this," she said, before moving her finger across a small black panel beside the door. A green fingerprint appeared briefly, before the panel swung aside to reveal some hidden buttons. "Your fingerprints are programmed in already," Granny said, pressing the bottom button.

"Where did you get our prints from?" Jessica asked.

"Mr. Yamamoto lifted them from the door handles of your rooms," Granny said, as if this was the most normal thing in the world.

"Where are we going, *obaasan*?" said Josh.

"Are we going to help Team O find Kiki?" Jessica asked, hopefully.

"Certainly not!" Granny said. "I have not changed my mind – you are far too young to be able to help. There are Yakuza involved; these are dangerous people."

"But we can't just do nothing now that we know all about it," Jessica protested.

"Precisely," said Granny. The lift doors swooshed open to reveal a long corridor – another mix of the modern and traditional. It was lit with bright halogen light bulbs and floored with traditional tatami mats. "We cannot ignore the fact that you are now involved," Granny continued, leading the way down the corridor. "As much as I would rather you had never found out about Team O. Now, because you know, you are in danger."

Josh felt the back of his neck prickle. He wouldn't be having this conversation with his cucumber-sandwich-eating, allotment-obsessed other grandparents back in England – or, Josh wondered, maybe he shouldn't be so quick to assume.

They came to the end of the corridor and a flight of steep stairs. Granny took them two at a time. Josh and Jessica looked at each other and followed. Josh thought of himself as being pretty fit – he could go four rounds with Jessica in their karate class and hardly break a sweat. But he was definitely getting a bit out of breath by the time they neared the top of the stairs. Granny was totally composed, not a silver hair out of place.

They emerged inside a bare wooden room with large shuttered windows all around it. Stepping outside, Josh realized the stairs had come up in an ornamental temple in the park that was just round the corner from the Sakura Apartments. They were separated from the rest of the park by a thick line of cherry trees and a pond. Josh walked up to the edge of the pond and a glimmer of golden movement caught his eye. A shoal of koi were swimming lazily just under the surface.

Granny walked up to a tree, opened a concealed panel in the bark and pressed her finger to the pad. Josh stepped back quickly as the surface of the pond rippled and then drew back underneath the grass, carp and all, to reveal a trapdoor that swung open into a deep hole.

Josh peered down the hole. It was a sheer drop –

he couldn't tell how deep it was, but he could see something blue at the bottom.

"Follow me," Granny said, and she stepped gracefully into the hole and disappeared.

Josh and Jessica exchanged shrugs and jumped. Cold air whipped past Josh and it all went dark for a few seconds before suddenly space opened up all around them and they found themselves falling through a huge underground chamber and onto a large, bouncy blue crash mat. Jessica giggled as she rolled off the crash mat. Josh got to his feet and jumped after her.

Granny Murata was standing beside the mat with her arms folded, waiting for them to join her. Josh looked around, and found they were in a cavernous room that had the crash mat at its centre and four corridors leading off in different directions. But unlike Team O's control room, this space was filled with people. Men and women in suits, martial arts uniforms and even riot gear bustled about, crossing the room from doorway to doorway.

"They don't seem bothered that there are two kids down here," Jessica observed, as Granny led them down one of the corridors.

"This is a top secret government facility, of which Team O is only a small part," said Granny smoothly. "My grandchildren dropping in are the least of their worries."

Everyone who passed bowed respectfully to Granny, even the giant man in anime-style mecha battle gear with what looked like a rocket launcher strapped to each arm.

"*Ohayō gozaimasu*, Murata-san," he said, his huge suit of armour clanking.

Finally they reached a double door at the end of the corridor, and Granny threw it open. Josh gasped. He'd expected more screens and dials, gleaming high-tech robotics – instead they seemed to be transported back into the samurai dojos of ancient Japan, but on a massive scale. There were tatami mats on the floor, kanji paintings on the walls, and martial artists practising their skills. As Granny led them across the room, they passed two black belts sparring, aiming swift kicks to each other's heads. Their high-kicking style told Josh they were probably tae-kwon-do experts.

"This is *so cool*," Jessica whispered to Josh.

"Imagine if Sensei Neil could see this? He'd have a fit!"

"Through here," said Granny, gesturing to a sliding door to their right, "You will find uniforms to fit you. You have five minutes to get changed. And then," she said, "your training will begin."

"So, can we learn to fight with any of these?" Josh asked, glancing at the racks of weapons laid out along the side of the dojo. There were staffs, daggers, pairs of nunchakus and wooden tonfa with their polished handles, even a row of gleaming katanas.

"No," said Granny Murata. "Hand-to-hand only. Weapons are only tools – it is no use picking up a weapon if your body is not absolutely under your control. Now, I believe you have had *some* training in London."

"Yes, *obaasan*," Jessica said. "We attend classes… once a week."

"Hmm," said Granny, unimpressed. "I am going to teach you ways to escape an attacker. Remember, the first thing you should do if you are in danger is run away and call for help. If you cannot do that, perhaps this will be useful. Josh, stand there. Don't move. I will be your attacker." She started to walk around him, moving slowly and silently, graceful and catlike. Josh planted his feet as firmly on the floor as he could and didn't move his head to follow her. He could sense her moving, was aware of the distance between them. He followed the shift of Jessica's eyes as she watched where Granny was going. He judged he had a few more seconds until she was—

Ack!

Suddenly Granny's arm was around his throat. He felt her arm pressing against his windpipe and had to concentrate not to start hyperventilating. He twisted his head to one side, to ease some of the pressure.

"Good," Granny said. "Now, try to free yourself." Josh kicked back with one leg and then the other, but Granny neatly sidestepped. He put his hands up to try to pull her arm away, and then hesitated. "Do not hold back, Josh, you cannot possibly hurt me," she said. He grabbed her arm and pulled. It was like iron, totally immovable. He could feel the muscles beneath her sleeve. How could his frail grandmother have body tone like this?

Finally, she let him go.

"Now," she said, "Look at my arm." Josh turned as she held her arm up, rolling the sleeve up to her elbow. "Somewhere in my grip there is a slack point," she said, clenching and unclenching her fist. "There is always some place in a person's grip that you can exploit. In almost all cases, grabbing an attacker's little finger will trigger their slack point and cause their grip to fail." She moved like lightning and then she suddenly had Josh by the throat again. "Try it," she said. Josh reached for the little finger of Granny's hand and pulled. To his amazement, he felt the muscles in her arm twitch and then relax, and he stepped out of her grip as easily as if he was shrugging off his jacket.

Next, Granny stood back and asked them to spar with each other.

"I wish to see what they teach in London," she said. Josh and Jessica found a space on the floor and bowed to Granny, and then each other. Josh took up his ready stance and nodded.

For a second, neither of them moved. Then Jessica hit out with her right hand, aiming squarely for his chest. He dodged, grabbed her hand and tried to pull her into a throw. But too late, he realized she was going with it, throwing all her weight into it and holding on to his arm so that she rolled straight onto her feet and he was thrown over backwards. He hit the mat with a thud and all the breath rushed out of his lungs. He'd fallen badly. He risked a glance at Granny. Her face was almost blank but she gave Jessica a tiny nod.

Frustrated, Josh stood and dusted himself down, determined to get a hit in on Jessica. Sure enough, she came at him again, but she was just a bit too cocky, and when she threw a high kick to her left he ducked under it and placed a back kick solidly to the middle of her back. She stumbled forwards but didn't go down. He followed it up with a low punch to the stomach but she turned and blocked and then he realized she'd grabbed his hands and she was trying to push them up so she could get a chest hit in. They struggled together for a moment, and then Josh saw Jessica's eyes flicker over to Granny Murata.

Now's my chance! He twisted his hands away to break her grip and got two good hits in on her chest with his elbow and the flat of his hand. Jessica backed off, gasping. Josh relaxed and shook out his shoulders, which was a bad idea because Jessica suddenly leaped into a jumping high kick. The sole of her shoe swept past Josh's face, millimetres from his nose.

"That's enough," said Granny. They both turned to look at her. She wasn't looking at them – she was reading the screen of a small gadget she had pulled out of a concealed pocket. "I have a message from Nana-san. I must go to work." She looked up. "You both have much work to do to improve. But I must admit, your skills are...serviceable. For now." Josh and Jessica grinned and then bowed to each other. "You both show promise. Indeed, together you could be a quite formidable team – in twenty to thirty years' time, after some extensive training. For now, you're good enough to look after yourselves if you need to."

They got changed back into their normal clothes, and when they came out of the changing rooms they found Granny had also changed out of her black Team O uniform and into the traditional lilac kimono.

When they arrived back at the central space with the big blue crash mat, Granny opened a panel in the wall and pressed some buttons.

"Does that call an elevator to get us back up there?" Josh asked, squinting up at the square of blue sky opening up above him as the surface of the pond slid back again.

"No," said Granny. As Josh watched, something dropped down the hole, twisting and uncoiling as it went. It was a rope.

"We're going to climb back up?" Jessica asked.

"It will be good for your arms," said Granny, in the same tone of voice as she always used to tell them to eat their vegetables. "And you know there is no danger."

"Not unless Jess falls on top of me," Josh muttered.

Chapter Seven

Granny was already nearly at the top of the rope by the time Jessica had found a way to pull her weight off the floor. Josh looked up. The square of daylight seemed a very long way away. He grabbed hold and pulled his legs up. His arms started to ache almost straight away. Jessica wasn't doing much better. She was only a couple of metres above and groaning with the effort. It wasn't long before the muscles in Josh's shoulders were trembling and his fingers burned with the strain of holding on to the rope. But he thought of Mr. Yoshida's Yakuza goons coming up behind them with their samurai swords, and managed to make himself keep going.

Finally he came to the top, grabbed onto the handhold imbedded in the ground at the edge of the pond, and half-hauled, half-rolled himself onto the grass. By the time he'd made it Jessica was already standing up, massaging her forearms with a pained expression on her face.

"I will be performing reconnaissance," Granny said, as Josh staggered to his feet. "My first step will be to follow that bodyguard. Nana-san has been examining his movements, and we think we know where he is going. You can return to my apartment. You will be safe there."

Jessica frowned at her shoes. Josh thought he could tell what she was thinking – with Team O on the case, it shouldn't feel like abandoning Kiki if they just did as they were told. But it *did* feel like that.

"No," he said.

"Excuse me?" Granny frowned at him.

"We can't just hide in the apartment," Josh went

on. "We helped you before, by following that bodyguard – and you've seen we can look after ourselves. You have to let us help."

"I cannot allow that," Granny said. "I appreciate your passion, but—"

"We can be useful to you," Jessica said. "We can be…Team O in training. The next generation of agents."

"Out of the question!" Granny said. "I'm surprised you would even ask me. Imagine what your parents would say if you were hurt."

"But we won't go rushing into danger," Jessica insisted. "I absolutely promise that we won't do anything you don't want us to do – but we have to do *something*." She looked Granny in the eye. "I know we only met her yesterday, but Kiki's our friend. We can't abandon her to the Yakuza. And – and if you won't let us help you where you can keep an eye on us, we *will* investigate on our own, and you can't stop us."

Josh nearly choked. *Argh, Jess*, he thought, *did you have to make that sound so much like a challenge?*

Granny stood very still for a moment. She looked at

Jessica, and then at Josh. Then something happened that Josh was totally not expecting. She smiled.

"You would risk yourselves for the life of a friend you have only known for a few hours," she said. "That is foolish. But it is also very honourable." She nodded. "Perhaps we can find you some way to help us. Indeed," she added to herself, "a family outing may be a good cover for this location. But you are *only* to go where I tell you, keep watch and listen for any suspicious conversations. And you must never tell your parents of any of this."

"*Hai!*" Josh and Jessica chorused.

"Very well. Come with me."

"Granny," Josh asked, as they got back into the lift and Granny Murata pressed the button for the lobby. "Where are we going?"

He watched as a smile spread over his Granny's face. "To sing some karaoke."

An hour later, Josh found himself in a glass elevator zooming up the side of a skyscraper with Jessica, Granny, and three elderly ladies.

"These are my neighbours, Miou-san, Yoshiko-san and Hina-san," Granny Murata had said, when they all met up in the Sakura Apartments. Then, while Miou, Yoshiko and Hina had their backs turned, Granny had continued. "They are ordinary ladies from the building, not members of Team O. They are karaoke enthusiasts," she whispered. "Their singing should provide enough cover for me to slip out and look for the bodyguard. You two will stay with me – you may be able to sneak in somewhere where I would be noticed."

Josh gazed out of the elevator at the centre of Tokyo spreading out beneath them, with its gleaming skyscrapers, crowded shops and ancient shrines all huddled together. The elevator finally reached the thirtieth floor and the doors swooshed open to reveal a reception area, with marble flooring and arty black and white photographs of singers hanging on the walls. Jessica looked at him and mouthed a silent "*Oooh!*" Josh nodded. This was one of those really swish karaoke lounges he'd heard about – very expensive, very serious, and a billion miles away from the raucous fun of the karaoke club the Murata family sometimes visited in London.

The receptionist ticked the group off on her list and gave them directions to their private room. They went through a pair of double doors and found themselves in a large, plush lobby with a deep maroon carpet and leather sofas next to massive flower arrangements in antique vases. There was no sign of the bodyguard.

The civilized atmosphere was shattered, though, by a loud wailing noise. It was coming from a teenage girl with bright pink pigtails, who was performing into a microphone on a small stage in the centre of the room. The wail eventually settled on a recognizable note, and the girls who surrounded the stage squealed and applauded madly.

"She's not that good," Josh muttered.

"That's Yoko Yay," Jessica told him under her breath.

Josh shrugged. "Don't know that one."

"You're probably better off. She's *mega*-rich, ultra-spoiled, and talentless! She's top of her class in throwing diva tantrums and falling out of limousines, but her singing is horrid."

They followed Granny down the corridor to their

private room. Miou, Hina and Yoshiko immediately crowded around the two touch-screen displays that showed the song choices. Before Josh knew what was happening Hina was up on the miniature stage, giving a half-English, half-Japanese performance of "Fly Me to the Moon".

The three ladies were taking it all so seriously, and the setting was so cultured, that Josh started getting nervous – what if they wanted him to do a song? What if, even worse, they actually expected him *to be able to sing*?

Sure enough, a few minutes later he found a microphone thrust into his hand and everybody looking at him expectantly. He went over and stared at the song list, but it was no good – all the songs he had ever known had flown out of his head.

"I know!" said Jessica, leaning across him and tapping the screen. "Yellow Submarine!" The familiar chords started up and Jessica grabbed a microphone and launched into the first verse. Josh shot her a grateful look and joined in, and soon he realized he was actually having fun. The old ladies were nodding along happily, and he thought he even saw Granny Murata smile.

When they'd finished, Granny stood up.

"Josh, Jessica, will you come with me?" she asked. "We passed a window with a beautiful view of the city – I'd like to show you some temples we might visit later today."

Josh and Jessica jumped to their feet. Time for ninja action!

"Please excuse us," Josh said, bowing to the ladies.

"Have a nice time," said Yoshiko cheerily. "Now whose turn was it?"

"Ooh, mine I think," said Miou, belting out the opening bars of "What's New Pussycat?".

Josh and Jessica slipped out after Granny. Out in the corridor, she reached into a pocket and pulled out a gizmo with a small screen and a dial. She beckoned the twins closer, and they drew around her, watching as she switched the dial to "receive". The screen filled with static, and then resolved into the smiling face of Nana, Team O's youthful surveillance expert.

"Good afternoon, Mimi," said Nana. "I've tapped into the CCTV in the karaoke bar. Yoshida must be rewarding the bodyguard handsomely for his treachery. He's been living it up all afternoon." Her face disappeared, replaced by grainy surveillance footage of the hulking shape of Kiki's bodyguard disappearing into one of the other private rooms. "Unfortunately," Nana's voice went on, "we have no visual access inside the room, so we don't know if he's alone. Be careful."

Granny nodded, and switched off the device.

"Stay here," she told Josh and Jessica. "I will investigate."

She shuffled slowly down the corridor, past all the doors to the private rooms, putting on an exaggerated old-lady walking speed so she had plenty of opportunity to look inside each room as she passed. As the twins watched, she suddenly turned around and strode back towards them.

"I have found him," she said. "He is in room 1, the VIP room. Unfortunately, he has company – two more of Yoshida's associates and a group of young ladies singing to them."

"Are we gonna bust in and pull him out?" Josh asked.

"No," Granny said. She gestured to her kimono. "It may have been a mistake to come here under cover.

I cannot fight properly in this kimono – and I cannot risk changing into my Team O uniform in public."

"Well – maybe you don't have to go in there at all," Josh said slowly. "If we can get him to follow us out of the building…there was that alley next door, right? Then we…"

"We?" Granny asked, raising an eyebrow.

"Well, okay," Josh said. "*You* could tackle him on your own and get him to tell us where they've hidden Kiki."

"Right – we could lure him out!" said Jessica, her eyes shining. "He knows us – and he really doesn't like us. If we burst in on him and then run for it, I'm sure he'll follow."

"I do not like this plan," said Granny. Josh's face fell. But then Granny nodded. "But it will work. And we must find Kiki quickly. Go back inside and sing one more song. That will give me time to change in private and prepare to ambush the bodyguard. Try to get him downstairs as quickly as possible." She hurried off.

Just as she was disappearing, a high-pitched squeal made Josh and Jessica turn.

"OH. My. *GAAHD!*" Yoko Yay and her gang of teenage girls were coming down the hall towards them. Yoko was waving her mobile phone madly. "It's finally happened!" Yoko was skipping down the hall. "I just got the call! I have to go right now to get ready for my *live studio recording*. *Banzai! Banzai!*" She did a couple of dance moves on the spot, and then looked around at her entourage. "I guess *some* of you can come backstage..." she said. At once there was a commotion of chatter from the girls.

"Oh, me!"

"Yoko, pick me!"

"No, me, me!"

Josh pressed himself against the wall to let them pass. None of them gave him a second glance – or even a first one. "At last, Grandpa's come through for me," Yoko clutched her mobile phone to her chest.

The crowd passed by and disappeared around a corner. Josh brushed himself down. "Come on," he said, "let's get back in there and get on with the plan."

But Jessica didn't move – she was frozen to the spot, staring after Yoko. "Josh!" she said. "Yay's not her real name!"

"Well, no," said Josh. "Sounds like a stupid stage name to me…"

"But Josh, her real name is *Yoshida*."

Josh stared at her. "…You think Mr. Yoshida is Yoko Yay's grandfather?"

"The leader of the Iron Fist – the one who has Kiki!" Jessica grabbed his arm. Josh felt a chill run down his spine as it all started to fall into place. Yoko's ambition, the sabotaged pop stars… "And, *and*, she was saying *banzai*!"

"Of *course*!" Josh said. "*Banzai Banzai Benzaiten!* Mr. Yoshida kidnapped Kiki so Yoko can take her place on that new music show."

"They are *not* going to get away with this," Jessica hissed, opening the door to their private room.

"You're right, Jess," Josh replied. "We're not going to let them."

"Ah, Josh-kun, Jessica-chan. Did you have a nice look at the view?" Hina asked, as they stepped inside.

"Oh yes, it's fantastic," said Josh.

"Where is Mimi?" Yoshiko said.

"She's just gone to the bathroom," said Jessica smoothly.

"Well, it's your turn," said Hina, handing Jessica the microphone. Josh and Jessica nodded to each other, and Josh checked his watch. About four minutes, then Granny would be ready for them to lure the bodyguard out of his room. Jessica went to the song list and picked something, and a few seconds later a familiar base line kicked in and Josh grinned at her. It was that song of Kiki's – *"Kumo no ue no ai"*!

Despite feeling the beginnings of a nervous twitch, Josh threw himself into the song. Then it was over, and Jessica and Josh bowed to the three old ladies.

"Excuse me," Josh said to Hina. "Could I please borrow your camera? The view from the window was so beautiful – I would love to go back and take a picture."

"Of course," Hina said, taking her digital camera out of its case and handing it over.

"I thought we could try to take his picture," Josh whispered after they'd left the room and shut the door behind them.

"Good idea," Jessica said. "He'll *hate* that."

"I just hope the camera's still in one piece at the

end of this," Jessica whispered as they crept up the corridor towards the VIP suite.

"I just hope *we* are!" Josh muttered back, checking the camera flash. "Three, two, one – go!"

They pushed open the door to the VIP suite and Josh raised the camera, pressing the button over and over again. *Snap snap snap snap snap snap.*

The group of girls cringed away from the camera and squealed, and the bodyguard and Yoshida's goons blinked in surprise.

"There he is!" Jessica cried. "There's Kiki's bodyguard!"

"You again!" the bodyguard roared, and he leaped to his feet.

"Go!" Josh yelled. They bolted down the corridor. He glanced over his shoulder and saw that yes, the bodyguard was following them – and so were the other two Yakuza thugs.

Josh and Jessica ran through the lobby and past the receptionist, and Josh pounded the "down" button on the elevator.

Nothing happened. There was no noise of the elevator wheels moving; no lights flashing.

"Oh, come on!" Josh snapped. A smashing noise made them both turn – the bodyguard was crashing through the lobby with the goons in his wake, upsetting the leather sofas and antique vases.

"Come on, come on..." Josh jabbed the button again as the receptionist shrieked and sprinted to catch a falling vase. The bodyguard was storming closer.

A uniformed staff member leaped in front of the bodyguard.

"Excuse me, what do you think you're—" The bodyguard shoved him aside.

"Take the stairs!" Jessica snapped, diving for a door on the other side of the room. Josh followed, and they started down a concrete stairwell, Jessica taking the lead. Josh peered over the edge of the banister – the drop seemed to go on for ever.

Suddenly a terrible thought struck Josh.

"Jess!" he said, swinging around a corner as the door banged open above them.

"What?" Jessica shouted back. There were heavy footfalls on the stairs.

"How will we get to the alleyway now?"

"...Don't know!" Jessica said. "Just keep running!"

Chapter Eight

Josh flew down the stairs. Just ahead of him Jessica grabbed the banister to pivot around another corner and kept on going. Josh ran until his legs felt stiff, then until they felt like jelly, then until he couldn't feel anything any more. Josh didn't know what floor they'd reached; he didn't even know how close the two goons were to catching him. He just kept running.

Finally, they hit the last set of stairs. A flash of black caught his eye. He turned to look, misjudged the corner, and ran smack into a wall. When lights stopped flashing in front of his eyes, he looked up and saw the lithe silhouette of Granny Murata swing across the stairwell and into the two Yakuza thugs that were following them, knocking them off their feet.

The bodyguard was clattering down the stairs towards Josh, his face red with rage. He grabbed for Josh's throat but he ducked away and the bodyguard ended up punching the wall.

"Argh!" he groaned, cradling his hand. He turned on Josh. "You little—" Josh backed away, but before the bodyguard could make another grab for him Jessica appeared, sprinting back up the steps to their landing. She cannoned into the bodyguard with her shoulder. He staggered, but recovered quickly and got an arm around her neck. Josh tried to land a kick on the back of the man's knees, hoping they'd buckle, but the bodyguard used Jessica like a shield. She let out an angry choking noise, and scrabbled with her hands on his arm as her face turned red.

Suddenly the bodyguard yelped – Jessica had found his little finger and pulled with all her might. His grip came loose and she scrabbled out from beneath his arm and ran over to Josh. The bodyguard looked at them with eyes full of loathing. Josh knew what to do, without even glancing at Jessica. In unison they spun around and placed two high kicks in their enemy's face. There was the snap of bone breaking. He fell down, out cold.

"Josh, Jessica – you are all right." Josh looked up to see Granny Murata descending the stairs two at a time.

"Granny!" they both cried out. Looking up, Josh could see two figures spread out on the concrete floor of the landing above them. Groaning and rolling from side-to-side, they had clearly taken a battering. Granny looked down at the bodyguard, whose huge limbs spread out around their feet. She nodded slowly, looking him up and down.

"Your technique is still in need of improvement," she commented. "But your improvisational skills are good." Josh and Jessica grinned at each other.

Josh kneeled down, turned the bodyguard over and rummaged in his jacket pocket. He found a wallet and a mobile phone.

"These should help," he said, passing the wallet

and phone to Granny. He turned back to the bodyguard and checked him for other pockets, or any kind of clue. He pulled the man's jacket open. That was funny – the lining was black silk, apart from one white seam. He pulled on the silk and the seam split open. A hidden pocket! And there was something inside...

"I've found something," he said, pulling out a small folded-up piece of paper.

"What is it?" Jessica asked.

"Dunno – it looks like a ticket for something. Why would he hide this?" He squinted at the letters. "Tokyo Tower...*Ro Ningyokan*."

Jessica's eyes lit up. "That's the waxworks museum – you remember Kiki said she was going there? That can't be a coincidence."

"No," Josh said, his heart beating even faster. "It's better than that – Mr. Yoshida owns a load of museums, right, Granny? Is this one of them?"

"It is," said Granny, raising her eyebrows. "You two are sharp thinkers. You believe Kiki might be hidden there?"

"Well, it's a public place. Mr. Yoshida can control the security, and Kiki loves to go there."

"Plus the bodyguard said on the phone that everyone would be able to see her," Jessica added.

"That is very plausible," said Granny Murata. She switched on a walkie-talkie. "Nana, can you call up activity outside the waxworks museum on the day Kiki was kidnapped?"

"I'm on it."

It was just a couple of moments before Nana's voice came back. "I've got Kiki's bright yellow electric hybrid car pulling up to the museum about an hour after she got off the plane."

"That confirms it. Good work, everybody," Granny said. "Team O will investigate the museum."

"We're coming with you," Jessica said.

"Please, Jessica – this is a serious matter. If you are right, the place may be filled with Yakuza."

"But it's a tourist attraction, and we're tourists! It's a brilliant cover," Josh argued.

"Exactly," Jessica agreed. "What's more natural than seeing the waxworks with your grandchildren – your unruly, curious grandchildren who have a tendency to open doors marked Staff Only?"

Granny Murata sighed. "*If* you do precisely as I say,

and *if* you promise me you will stay safe, and *if* you remember your training..." She hesitated. Josh held his breath.

C'mon, Granny, he thought. *We don't have much time!*

"Then, it looks like we will be paying a family visit to the waxworks museum this summer," Granny said. Josh had to clench his fists to stop himself from whooping for joy. He and Jessica bowed respectfully to Granny, and then high-fived behind her back as they stepped over the unconscious bodyguard and started down the steps.

"What about your friends?" Jessica asked. "Are they still singing karaoke? Should we go and get them?" Josh remembered that they'd left the three old women in the booth.

"Don't worry about them," Granny reassured her. "I phoned Hina's mobile phone to say we've been called away, and I'd return her camera when I see her tomorrow." She held out her hand and Josh dug the camera out of his pocket. To his dismay, the screen was cracked. It must have happened when he ran into the wall.

"I'm so sorry, Granny – I'll pay for it," he promised.

"Well – that is very honourable of you," said Granny Murata. "But I'm sure Sachiko can fix it in the Team O workshop."

The Tokyo Tower was an old radio tower that had been turned into a tourist attraction. It was shaped like the Eiffel Tower, painted in orange and white stripes. Josh leaned up against the passenger window as their car pulled up to the front of the four-storey building that sat at its centre. One of the tower's legs passed them by, with its massive steel latticework gleaming in the late afternoon sunlight. He and Jessica had been there once before – one summer their parents had brought them to Tokyo and they'd gone to the special observatory at the top, and had totally failed to see Mount Fuji on the horizon because it had been too cloudy. But it had been an awesome day anyway.

The car stopped, and the doors opened. Josh climbed out to see five ancient people standing in front of him, wrapped in warm clothes and leaning on sticks. If he hadn't already seen it with his own eyes, he never would have believed that Nakamura, Sachiko, Nana, Mimasu and Mr. Yamamoto were capable of standing up straight, let alone fighting off armies of Yakuza. Now, they looked ancient. Mr. Yamamoto was carrying a backpack that looked like it might topple him over at any minute. Granny Murata adopted her own elderly body language as soon as she stepped out of the car, bending over and taking small, shuffling steps and nodded curtly to the others.

They entered the building, which was swarming with tourists and locals. Josh spotted two TV screens showing the early evening news. A scrolling subtitle said *Chiba Mikiko still missing – bodyguard found assaulted in stairwell, two known Yakuza arrested*. Granny ushered the group into the lifts.

"Keep your eyes open for anything suspicious, any heavily guarded areas or hidden doors," Granny told the rest of Team O as the lift whirred up to the third floor. "Thanks to Josh and Jessica, now we know what Yoshida's up to." Josh felt his face flush with pride as Sachiko and Nana both grinned at them. "If we do not find Kiki within an hour and a half, Yoko will take her place on her new music show – and we do not know what will happen to Kiki after that."

The wax museum was impossible to miss – the doorway was painted bright yellow and the president of America was standing outside with three members of the Beatles. A sign on the wall said "Apologies – John Lennon removed for cleaning."

Granny hobbled up to the counter and bought a group ticket for them. "I am here with my English grandchildren," she told the girl at the counter.

"Awww – *kawaii!*" The girl beamed at Josh and Jessica.

"Yes," Granny said, looking every bit the sweet, twinkly-eyed grandmother. "They are *kawaii*, aren't they?"

Josh wasn't sure about being called *kawaii* – it was like "cute", but with an extra veneer of sickly sweet adorableness.

They went into the museum through a group entrance. Nana pulled a shiny gadget from her pocket. "There are twelve surveillance cameras in this museum," she whispered to the others. "So there will be certain times when we need to tread carefully – we will almost certainly be watched."

"Let's make sure our cover holds up," Mimasu added under her breath. "Plenty of shuffling. I'll be stone deaf; Nakamura-san, you can be nearly blind."

A young lady in a red blazer met them in front of the first room.

"*Ohayō!*" she chirruped, handing them all leaflets about the museum. "I am Mandi! I will be your guide for today!"

Sachiko immediately engaged her in conversation.

She'll keep her occupied, Josh thought, *while we investigate*.

Mandi led them through a set of doors into a room full of European royalty, including a wax sculpture of England's crown jewels. The room was almost empty of other visitors. Josh supposed the museum might be winding down for the night. It would be shutting soon. Josh looked around for anything that could be suspicious – hidden doors, obvious security cameras, roped-off areas – but he couldn't see anything. Mimasu beckoned him over to take a picture of Mr. Yamamoto with the Queen.

Josh sidled up to Jessica, who was examining a slightly wonky version of Prince Philip. "See anything?"

"Nothing," she said. "Except that I think the prince's wig might be on the wrong way round."

They kept their eyes open, but after a few more rooms, Josh started to get jumpy. There seemed to be nothing here except waxworks and tourists. *Where's Kiki?* he thought. If they didn't find her soon... Josh felt an involuntary shudder pass over him. He only hoped that their new friend's life wasn't in danger.

They passed through rooms celebrating the ancient emperors of Japan, the Japanese space programme, and Hollywood movie stars. The crowds of visitors got bigger and noisier. A loud group of American teenagers was gathered in the Hollywood room.

"Oh, take my photo with James Bond!" one of them cried.

"Ewww, Clark, quit kissing Superwoman; that's disgusting," shrieked another.

"Everything seems normal," Granny said to Nakamura, the noise of the teenagers covering their conversation.

"For a waxworks museum, anyway," Jessica added to Josh.

"And this is our music celebrity room," said Mandi, leading them into the biggest, loudest room yet. "Very popular, come inside and meet the stars."

People were forming queues to get their photos taken with their favourite singers, and a crowd had gathered around a large exhibit in the middle of the room. It was a four-poster bed, draped in silk and gauzy fabric that swayed gently as people passed by. And lying on the bed, as if she was fast asleep, was the waxwork of Kiki that she mentioned on the plane.

"*Oh*," said Jessica. "It's so realistic. It's set up just like her video for 'Dreaming of You'. Just look at that *dress*."

Josh was looking. The dress had to be about ten metres long, wrapping the waxwork in artful folds. It was made of some kind of shimmering cloth that changed colour as they walked around the display.

Team O spread out around the room. Mr. Yamamoto leaned close to Josh's ear.

"Mimi says to stay alert. It would be just like Mr. Yoshida to hide Kiki somewhere near here."

Josh looked around the room. There was a door marked Staff Only. Maybe Kiki was in there, hidden away from the public? He nudged Jessica and started to walk towards it, letting his path take them a couple of times round a blond pop star and in between the cast of a famous movie musical, until they were passing by the door.

"Ready?" Josh whispered to his sister. Jessica nodded, her face pale. Then he took a deep breath, grabbed the handle and flung the door open.

Chapter Nine

Josh braced himself for wailing alarms and the sight of Kiki tied to a chair, but he didn't get either. The room was a store cupboard, full of wigs, costumes and bits of waxwork, including a box of arms and a shelf of heads.

Beside him, Jessica sighed. "Good try," she said.

"Hey!" cried Mandi, rushing up to them. "Really, you cannot go in there."

"Josh, Jessica, you stop that this minute," said

another voice. Josh turned. Granny was smiling and bowing to Mandi. "Please excuse them, they are half-English. They're staying with me for the summer."

"Oh, well, please keep a better eye on them in future," Mandi said.

"I will," said Granny.

Mandi still looked a bit doubtful.

Mr. Yamamoto stepped up and bowed to her. "Mandi-san," he said, giving her a sparkling smile. "Have you ever thought of becoming an actress? I think you're far prettier than any of the figures here." Mandi giggled, completely distracted from Josh and Jessica.

"Keep looking," Granny murmured to Josh. "It was a good try – but it would be better if you try not to draw attention to yourselves again."

"Right," Josh said.

Mandi ushered Team O into the next room, which was much less crowded and seemed to have no particular theme. Mr. Yamamoto stuck by her.

They walked along a corridor and past a big metal door, with two burly men in black suits and sunglasses standing guard. One of the guards fixed Josh with a suspicious glare as they passed.

"I'm reading lots of human activity through there," Sachiko whispered when they were out of range. She showed Josh and Jessica her camera – the screen showed a heat-sensitive scan of the area around them. "Lots of body heat behind that door."

"That *has* to be where they're keeping Kiki," said Jessica. "But how can we get in?"

"Follow our lead," Sachiko said.

They came to the end of the tour and found themselves approaching the exit to the museum. Mandi left them to find their way out, bowing to the women and letting Mr. Yamamoto kiss her hand. After she was gone, Mr. Yamamoto and Granny Murata split from their group, waving the other four members of the team off and beckoning Josh and Jessica to follow them into a bathroom.

Inside the bathroom, where there weren't any security cameras, Mr. Yamamoto opened up his backpack and pulled out four piles of clothing.

"The museum will be shutting down for the night very soon," Granny Murata said. "The others are going straight to the TV studio, to see if they can stall the music show and give us more time to find Kiki. Nana has provided us with disguises, so we can keep looking."

"Here's your cleaner's outfit, Josh," said Mr. Yamamoto, passing him some blue overalls and a black T-shirt. "And yours, Jessica." Jessica's disguise looked exactly the same. "And to hide the fact that you are twins – here." He passed Josh a baseball hat.

"Quickly, please," Granny Murata interrupted.

Josh went into one of the bathroom cubicles and climbed into his disguise, and when he stepped out, he saw Jessica's feet disappearing into the ceiling. Mr. Yamamoto held a square of ceiling tile and Granny Murata was standing on the sink counter.

Josh climbed up on the sink counter next to her. She kneeled and took one foot in her hand, and then gave him a boost-up so he could cling on to the inside of the ceiling. Then, after Mr. Yamamoto had followed, Granny swung herself in and pulled the ceiling tile up after her.

"It's very dark," Jessica commented.

"Aha," said Mr. Yamamoto. "Try squeezing the top

button of your uniform." Suddenly a bright light illuminated the dusty space.

"Wow!" Jessica breathed. "Buttons that double as torches!"

"Good old Sachiko," Mr. Yamamoto grinned. "She thinks of everything."

"That way," Granny said, pointing across the ceiling to a place where a thin sliver of light was seeping through. They crawled towards it. Josh tried to move quickly, but not so quickly that he sent clouds of dust up – he was in severe danger of sneezing with every breath. Finally they found that the light was coming through a metal grille that looked down on one of the waxwork rooms.

"The museum is now closed," said a robotic voice somewhere below them. *"Thank you for visiting the waxworks museum. Please come back soon."* They waited. A few people passed by underneath them.

"Thank you for visiting, but you must leave now," one of the guards said, marching two teenage girls towards the exit. Their protests faded away as they turned the corner.

"Aw, just one more photo? Please…?"

Finally, the lights went out, and everything went quiet.

"Let's go," Granny whispered. "We don't have long before the show begins." She levered up the grille and lowered herself into the room. Mr. Yamamoto followed her, moving nimbly, and between them they helped Josh and Jessica to climb down. Josh looked around. There were figures in the darkness. His heart started to beat faster. In his head, he knew that of *course* there were figures – they were in the middle of the waxworks museum. But the more he tried to see the shapes for what they were, just harmless lumps of wax, the more they looked like evil creatures, just waiting for him to look away before they leaped.

Granny rummaged in her pocket and brought out a larger torch, which she waved around at the still, silent figures. It cast deep shadows and threw a harsh spotlight onto blank, staring eyes and fixed smiles. Empress Jingū's benevolent smile suddenly looked far from friendly, as if she was thinking about a nice steaming plate of boiled Josh.

"This way," Granny said, and led them through the waxworks towards the door.

Something moved to Josh's right. He jumped and knocked into Jessica, and nearly let out a yell of alarm – but it was only David Beckham, kicking his football.

"You okay?" Jessica asked.

"I'm *fine*."

"Only, you seemed scared…"

"I was not scared," Josh whispered. "I was – startled. That's very different."

"If you say so."

"*Very* different."

"Please be quiet," said Granny Murata. Josh glared at Jessica and she stuck her tongue out at him.

They moved through the doorway and into another waxworks room.

Suddenly a light flared, and a burly figure stepped out.

"*Omaesan!* What are you doing there?" he demanded.

"Juno-san, I can still see rubbish behind Winston Churchill. Please pick it up," said Granny, making eye contact with Jessica and pointing. Jessica scurried off to sweep behind the waxwork, and Josh immediately started inspecting the underside of the closest waxwork's hand. Luckily – or maybe unluckily – he found some genuine chewing gum stuck there and pulled it off with a satisfied grunt. He noticed that Mr. Yamamoto was already on the other side of the room, wiping the dust off Steven Spielberg's nose.

"Huh?" said the security guard. "Why are you still cleaning at this hour?"

"The Boss," said Granny, wearily. "He is so demanding at the moment – you must have noticed." The security guard hesitated. Josh held his breath.

"Yeah," the guard said. "The Boss is a hard man to please. Like these new guards – I've been with the Boss for twenty years, suddenly this week he hires all new guys. *And* they're getting paid more than me."

"Exactly," said Granny. "So I am putting my team on double-shifts this week until it is finished. I want to make sure he has nothing to complain about from me."

"I don't blame you a bit," said the guard. "I'll leave you to it." He turned and walked back out the way he came.

Josh finally let out his breath.

"Whew," he said. "That was a close call."

"Wait here," said Granny, looking down the corridor that had the metal door. "The door is unguarded now."

Cautiously, they moved towards the door and Granny put her hand up to it, and then pressed her ear to it. "I hear nothing."

"Would they leave Kiki unguarded?" Jessica wondered.

"Ah, but she is very secure. Look," Granny said, leading them into the corridor. Josh wasn't sure what she meant until she pointed to the door. There was a keypad, but no handle.

"Oh, very clever," Mr. Yamamoto said, nodding in approval. He dug his hand into one of his pockets and pulled out a sleek black device. "But you have to be a bit cleverer than that to get the better of Team O!" He handed the device to Granny. "One of Mimasu's specials. This should get us past their entry code system. If it works."

"If?" Josh asked. Mr. Yamamoto shrugged.

"Well…it is quite experimental," he admitted. Granny Murata held the device up to the door.

For a moment, nothing happened. Then the screen on the device lit up. Numbers started to rush over the screen. Finally the numbers resolved into a string of twelve digits. Granny reached up and tapped the sequence of numbers out on the keypad. The door clicked and swung slightly inwards. Josh pushed it open.

"Kiki...?" he whispered.

But it was no good. The room held several chairs and tables, a large safe, a drinks cabinet...but no Kiki.

"*Shimatta!*" spat Mr. Yamamoto. "The Iron Fist gang must have just left – probably to go to the TV studio."

Josh's stomach turned over. Yoko Yay would have her breakthrough. Mr. Yoshida's gang would win.

"But – where's Kiki?" Jessica asked, very quietly. Josh knew that tone of voice. It was her there's-no-way-I'm-going-to-let-this-make-me-cry voice.

"We'll have to abort this mission," Granny said. "Kiki isn't here, and we can't get caught."

Josh looked around for any other clue as to where they might have taken her. He'd been so sure they were right about Kiki being here.

"We'll sneak out a side entrance, near the front door," said Granny.

The four of them hurried down the corridor and Josh felt more and more like they'd lost their only chance to find Kiki. Josh stomped ahead in frustration, almost not caring if they got caught, but when he passed the music stars room, he stopped short.

There was a strange red glow coming from around the doorway leading to that room. He ran up and tried to open the door. It was locked.

"Hey," he whispered to the others. "I think I've found something."

Granny came up to the door and examined it. "A normal lock – no experimental technology needed here," she said. She reached up and pulled a hairpin out of her bun. A few seconds of wiggling it in the keyhole, and the lock went *click*.

Josh opened the door and stared in amazement. The whole room was covered in security laser beams, like the ones they had in museums and palaces in the movies. They made it impossible to cross the room, and turned the Kiki waxwork's bed with its flowing silks a sickly dark pink colour.

"Why would they need so much security?" Josh asked. "How's it different to any other room?" Granny and Mr. Yamamoto peered inside, trying to see all around the walls without setting off any of the laser alarms. But Josh saw Jessica was staring straight ahead, directly at the Kiki waxwork.

"That waxwork just moved," Jessica whispered.

"It's just your eyes playing tricks," Josh said.

"No," Jessica insisted. "Kiki's waxwork moved."

"Jessica – you cannot be suggesting..." Granny began.

"I am! It is!" Jessica pointed to the waxwork. "That *is* Kiki!"

"It makes perfect sense," said Josh. "The bodyguard said she was somewhere everyone could see her. Not just in public, actually on display! What better way to hide someone than disguised as their own statue?"

A low moan came from the centre of the room and the fabrics on the bed shifted as a foot twitched.

The figure definitely was moving. They'd found Kiki!

Chapter Ten

"She must have been drugged," Jessica said, wringing her hands. "And it's starting to wear off."

"Chiba Mikiko," Granny whispered. "Can you hear me?" There was no reply, but Kiki rolled over and groaned. "We are going to get you out of here," Granny said. "Just hold on."

"We have to do something quickly," Josh said, a horrible thought striking him as Kiki wriggled again. "If she rolls off the bed in this state she could set off the alarm herself!"

Mr. Yamamoto sighed. "It looks like the only way to turn it off is to get to that switchboard." He pointed into the room. Josh had to strain his eyes to see in the dim light, but he eventually spotted a tiny metal panel attached to the wall in the corner of the room. "One of us must climb through these beams," Mr. Yamamoto said.

"Right," Granny Murata said, rolling up her sleeves.

"Wait," said Mr. Yamamoto. "We run a high risk of setting off the alarms – and the taller the person, the higher the risk. We need to send the smallest person."

"Yes, I see," said Granny. The two of them looked at Josh and Jessica, who looked at each other.

Josh's throat went dry, then he nodded.

"I'll go," he said. "After all, Jessica is always teasing me that I'm two centimetres shorter than she is."

Jessica looked like she was about to argue. Then she nodded. "It should be you," she said. Josh stepped forwards into the room. "Hey – good luck," Jessica added, stepping in with him as far as she could go without touching the beams of light.

"To avoid activating the alarm, you need to make sure you are aware of your whole body, Josh," Granny said.

Josh got down on his hands and knees to avoid the first beam and then approached the second beam at knee level. He lay down on his stomach and crawled underneath. Two down. He kept crawling. Sweat started to break out on his brow, and he tried to control his breathing without holding his breath.

He remembered being back in England, being in karate class, or in PE at school, or just running for a bus or climbing a tree. He used to pretend he was the hero of a comic book, and it always helped to put on that extra burst of speed or strength. It wasn't really helping now. Comic book heroes suddenly seemed like they had it easy.

"Careful," whispered Jessica. "Just above you." Josh ducked and turned to look. She was right, he'd come close to brushing a beam with the top of his head. He put his hand out behind him and gave her a thumbs up. Then he kept moving, looking around for larger spaces between the beams that he could crawl into and still get out of again. It felt like very slow going. Kiki moaned again, and Josh swallowed. He had to try to go faster.

"You are doing well," Granny Murata said. "Don't lose focus."

He kept moving forwards; there were only three beams left. He raised one foot carefully, twisted around for the second step and ducked for the third. Then with a final push, he threw himself forward. He'd made it! He stood up, leaning against the wall and stretching his limbs out.

"You did it!" Jessica said.

He examined the panel, hoping for an OFF button. But there was no OFF – or any other word or number that he recognized. His heart sank.

"Oh no. No, no!" he said. "It's in kanji. The buttons are all labelled in kanji; I can't read them."

"Josh," Granny Murata snapped. "Did I not *tell* you to keep up with your studies? This is what happens when you are slack about learning your mother tongue!" Josh thought about pointing out that as it was their dad who was Japanese, it was probably their father tongue. But this didn't really seem like the time.

"I'll have a look," said Mr. Yamamoto. Josh looked over to see that he was using his camera again. "I think it's the switch in the top left-hand corner."

"This one?" Josh pointed. "Are you sure?"

"Pretty sure," Mr. Yamamoto said.

Josh sighed. That would have to be good enough. He squeezed his eyes shut, and flicked the switch. An electronic droning noise filled his head and he covered his ears, bracing himself for wailing alarms. He'd run and grab Kiki and they'd fight their way out of the building...

Then something went *beep* and silence fell. Josh opened his eyes. The beams were fading away. Jessica jogged on the spot until they'd all vanished and then sprinted over to Kiki's bed, followed by Granny and Mr. Yamamoto.

"Kiki, I'm so glad you're all right!" Jessica cried. Kiki tried to sit up and rub her eyes, but she couldn't move very far – Jessica pulled back layers of fabric to find that she was tied to the bed. Granny and Mr. Yamamoto went to work on the knots, and finally Kiki managed to sit up. Jessica couldn't hold herself back – she threw her arms around her idol.

"Hey," Kiki said. "I know you, I think – you are from the plane? Jessica! And you had – hey, there you are," she said, groggily, spotting Josh.

"Yamamoto-san, call HQ and let them know that we have found Kiki and that she is safe," Granny ordered. Mr. Yamamoto pulled a mobile phone out of his pocket and nodded. "Kiki – do you remember what happened to you?"

"I thought – I thought it was a bit funny," Kiki muttered. "My agent didn't tell me I was appearing at the *Ro Ningyokan*…they wanted me there, as soon as I'd got off the plane, but…my agent didn't say anything. My bodyguard took me there…and then…I don't know what happened."

"Your bodyguard betrayed you. You were kidnapped. They hid you in the *Ro Ningyokan*, disguised as a waxwork!" Josh said. "But now everything's going to be fine."

"Yes," said Kiki, stretching out her arms. "I think so. I feel a lot better now. But why would anybody kidnap me?"

"It was an evil Yakuza boss," Josh said. "Yoko Yay's grandfather. He wants her to present *Banzai Banzai*

Benzaiten instead of you, so he kidnapped you and hid you away here."

"Oh…that *is* evil," said Kiki.

"Nana has been pushing back the time of the live recording," said Mr. Yamamoto, hanging up the mobile phone. "We have half an hour. We must go, right now."

Clap. Clap. Clap.

Josh spun around. Figures were moving slowly towards them through the gloom. Six big, burly figures and one smaller, thinner one. The thin man stopped his slow clapping and stepped into the room. Josh caught his breath. The thin face, the grey hair slicked back into a ponytail, his gold tooth glinting in the light from Granny's torch. It was him. It was Mr. Yoshida.

Chapter Eleven

"I'm really very impressed," said Yoshida, with a smile like a shark spotting its lunch. "You figured out my little trick. Perhaps I shall have mercy on you after all!" Suddenly he grabbed a gun from one of his goon's hands and fired. The bullet flew harmlessly into the floor, but the gunshot exploded like the sound of a cannon. Josh and Jessica both jumped and clenched their fists, and Kiki cringed away with a shriek. "Or perhaps not." Yoshida grinned.

"Yoshida-san," Granny Murata said, her voice perfectly calm, stepping forwards. "It is admirable that a grandfather should help his granddaughter achieve her dreams. But, like everything you do, you have gone about this the wrong way. Now, you will let Kiki go and take her rightful place at the recording." Yoshida and Granny Murata locked eyes. Then Yoshida walked up to her, getting much too close for Josh's liking.

"Mimi Murata," he said. "I should have guessed I would run into you again someday. How long has it been?"

"Not long enough, Noboru," said Granny.

Josh realized that these two must have a history. He wondered what secrets lay in Granny Murata's hidden ninja past.

"What a shame our reunion, like your friends, will be so very short-lived." Yoshida turned and walked back to his goons. "We need the singer alive for now," he said, strolling to the back of the group. "Her death must be made to look like an accident. Kill the rest how you like."

"Kiki, stay back," Granny ordered. "We will deal with this." Josh glanced back at Kiki. She nodded and backed up against the wall, half-hiding behind the waxwork of a famous girl band.

The goons moved forwards, drawing samurai swords from their belts. There was a deathly hush. Josh half-saw, half-felt Jessica tense beside him.

With a flourish, Granny Murata threw her arms out and two gleaming lengths of steel unfolded from her sleeves, clicking together to form two samurai swords. She threw them into the air in front of the twins – Josh caught one, Jessica the other.

"A present from Mimasu-san," she said, a grin spreading across her face. "Stay close, and watch your back!" Then with a cry she somersaulted into the middle of the group of Yakuza and caught two of them under the chin with her elbows. Mr. Yamamoto leaped after her, pulling a pair of nunchackus from the pocket of his overalls. They made a *whum whum whum* noise as he twirled them over his head, and then a satisfying *thunk* as they connected with one of the goons' knees.

"Josh, look out!" Kiki cried, as a thug with a jagged scar over his cheek raised his sword and sliced it through the air towards him. Josh brought his sword up just in time to block it.

"Split up," he said to Jessica. "Now!" He and Jessica threw themselves aside, one to the man's left and one to his right. The thug hesitated, not sure which of them to follow. Josh and Jessica dropped to the ground and rolled, coming up behind the man's back, and then spun into their twin-kick move and got a good blow in on the back of his head. He stumbled into the Britney Spears waxwork and they both crashed to the floor in a pile of cracked wax and blonde wig.

"He'll have another nasty scar," Jessica grinned.

Josh looked around. Granny was leaping from shoulder to shoulder across Yoshida's minions, avoiding swiping sword blades, while Mr. Yamamoto's nunchackus swung and smacked into the head of a man with bright blue hair, knocking him unconscious.

Josh grinned and turned to see how Kiki was doing, only to come face-to-face with the giant fist of a Yakuza thug coming straight towards him. He ducked, and as he came back up, Josh spotted a flash of grey out of the corner of his eye. He turned to see Yoshida dart past him and grab Kiki's arm, dragging her out from behind the waxwork.

"Granny, watc— *argk*!" A giant arm wrapped around

Josh's throat and pulled tight across his windpipe. Bright white dots flashed in front of his face as he watched Yoshida drag Kiki towards the door. The thug was going to pull his head right off his shoulders! Josh reached for his little finger and tried to pull it...but it didn't work. His grip didn't loosen a millimetre. What had Granny said? *There is always a slack place...* Josh felt all along the goon's arm. Desperately, he grabbed at the man's wrist and pulled.

"Argh!" the thug yelped. His arm fell away, and Josh grabbed the closest heavy object, a waxwork singer's microphone stand, and swung it at the man's head as hard as he could.

"You...little..." he began to say. Then his eyes rolled back in his head and he collapsed.

"Granny!" Josh yelled, sprinting after the disappearing Yoshida and Kiki. "He's got Kiki!"

Granny Murata looked around, placed a spinning high kick into the chest of a minion who had raised his sword to cut her in two, and followed.

Josh ran down the corridor and into the room of presidents and nearly stumbled over President Lincoln, who had fallen across the doorway. Yoshida and Kiki were at the other end of the room. Yoshida chuckled and placed a spinning kick to the neck of the nearest waxwork, sending its head flying one way and its body another. The pieces cannoned into others and one by one, like dominoes, the waxworks started to topple. Through the flurry, Josh saw Yoshida haul Kiki away.

He took a run-up and vaulted over Lincoln, weaving through the room, ducking and jumping as heavy wax statues fell all around him. He threw himself into a handstand to avoid a tumbling President Washington and sprang back onto his feet. He sprinted to the end of the room.

In the doorway he paused, looking back at the devastation. Granny appeared at the other side of the room.

"Keep going," she called, leaping up onto President Lincoln's back. "I will be just behind you!"

Josh turned and ran after Yoshida, getting to the lobby just in time to see the door to the stairwell bang shut.

Oh good, thought Josh. *Stairs again.*

He threw open the door to the stairwell and looked down, but there was no sign of them. He heard a scuffle above him and Kiki gave a little cry. Josh looked up and realized Yoshida wasn't going down and out – he was taking Kiki up, towards the roof.

"Stop!" Josh called, but Yoshida only laughed. Josh headed up after them, taking the stairs two at a time. After a few seconds he heard the stairwell door bang open again. He really hoped it was Granny.

At last, with his legs aching and his knees screaming, he reached the door to the roof and threw it open. A gust of cold wind ruffled his hair and he heard the sounds of traffic carrying up from the street below.

The roof of the building at the foot of Tokyo Tower had been converted into a giant playground. Massive metal statues of animals and cartoon characters loomed over swings and see-saws, and above it all sat the orange and white metal beams of the Tokyo Tower, lit by floodlights from below. Josh spotted Kiki's flailing arms disappearing behind a towering purple crocodile and sprinted after her. As he rounded the crocodile, Granny caught up to him and overtook – and then stopped so suddenly that Josh almost ran into her.

"Ah-ah-ah – I wouldn't come any closer if I were you, Mimi."

Yoshida had Kiki balanced precariously on the edge of the roof, holding her by the wrists so she couldn't grab onto him to stop herself from falling. His gun was trained on Granny. Kiki was sobbing, eyeliner running down her cheeks.

"Help me!" she cried. Josh's stomach turned over at the sight of Kiki in danger. He couldn't just stand there. He nearly started forwards but Granny put a firm hand on his shoulder.

"You won't do this, Noboru," said Granny. She started walking towards him, very slowly but very calmly.

"Oh, you think not?"

"I think not. It's not your style," Granny said. "Everything was always about money with you. Where is the benefit for you in killing an innocent singer?"

"Perhaps I'm branching out in my old age," Yoshida grinned. Granny kept on walking towards him. Yoshida glanced at Kiki, and Granny took the opportunity to look at Josh and nod slightly. Josh started to inch forwards, sure that Granny was about to make her move – whatever that was going to be. "I can drop her," Yoshida continued, pleasantly. "It'll look like she jumped – probably depressed because she was beaten to the TV show job by my granddaughter."

"You won't get away with this," Granny said. She was nearly within reach now. Yoshida laughed.

"Come now, Mimi, you know how this goes. This isn't one of those Hollywood movies. I am the most powerful businessman in all Japan. The police can't and won't touch a hair on my head."

"I have never liked your hair," said Granny.

"What—?" Yoshida began, confused, and Granny chose that moment to strike, feinting to the right and reaching around with her left hand to snatch the gun from Yoshida's hand and throw it off the roof. Josh moved forwards, but it was too late – Kiki let out an ear-piercing scream as Yoshida let go of her wrists. She was falling!

Chapter Twelve

Josh sprang across the roof and grabbed for Kiki, missing her arms, but catching her by the edge of one of her long, silky sleeves. The fabric started to rip but it hit a seam and held just long enough for him to grab her hand. She was screaming with fear and her flailing limbs didn't make Josh's task any easier.

"Keep still!" he urged her, as his muscles trembled with the effort of holding her weight. Kiki let out a final, muffled sob and managed to calm herself. Josh reached hand over hand, grasping her arm, then hooking a hand under an armpit until – yes! She collapsed onto the tarmacked roof beside him.

"You okay?" he asked.

"Yes, I think so," Kiki replied, her face pale.

"Give up, Mimi!" Yoshida cried. Josh spun around to see Granny and Mr. Yoshida fighting hand to hand. Their arms and legs were moving so fast they were almost a blur. As Josh watched, neither of them looked like they'd managed to actually hit the other at all – it was punch, block, elbow, block, block, block, block. Granny lashed out and grabbed one of Yoshida's wrists, holding it in an iron grip, but his other hand seemed to move twice as fast throwing more and more punches, and now Granny couldn't dodge as easily. She tried to throw him over her shoulder, but he just used the force of her throw against her, rolling as he hit the floor and sending her flying.

"I tire of this," Yoshida said. Granny was up again in seconds, but Yoshida was too fast for her, and he was off, sprinting along the edge of the roof and leaping up onto the orange metal struts of the tower. Despite the constraints of his shiny suit and slippery brogues, he was soon scrambling up them like a ladder. He sprang across to the next building.

"Granny, we have to go after him!" Josh cried, leaping to his feet and looking up to see if he could make the jump across. If he climbed higher up the tower and found some way to push himself off with enough force...

"No," said Granny Murata, coming up to Josh and grabbing him by the shoulders before he could run after Yoshida. "We do not have time for that right now."

Yoshida bowed and waved mockingly at Granny Murata. Then he caught Josh's eye.

Josh stared back. *This isn't over, Yoshida*, he thought. He was pretty sure this was not the first time the Murata family had seen off the Yakuza boss – and he was determined it wouldn't be the last.

"Let's get Kiki to this show. Are you able to go on, dear?" Granny asked, helping Kiki to her feet.

"Yes," she said, wiping her eyes on her sleeve. "I won't let Yoko go on in my place."

"Good!" Granny said with a smile. Her dentures glimmered white in the glare of the floodlights. "Let's get you to that studio." She spoke into a device on her wrist. "Yamamoto-san, we have Kiki. Is Jessica with you? Good. Meet us at the car." She pulled on her belt and two cords with clasps on the end spooled out. With an expert aim, she threw a small grappling hook into the air. It clamped on to one of the metal struts of the Tokyo Tower. Granny tugged it twice, then in a few swift movements she had clipped one cord onto Josh's belt, another onto Kiki's dress, and all three of them were moving towards the edge of the roof.

"Granny…!" Josh gasped, but barely had time to catch his breath before they had launched off the roof and into the air.

Time stood still as they hung there for a second – Josh could see the streets of Tokyo glittering all around them, and Team O's car down below, and Mr. Yamamoto and Jessica coming out of the building and looking up…Kiki's dress streamed out behind her in the breeze…and then they fell.

Josh's stomach seemed to stay behind on the roof as the ground rushed up to meet them. The wind tugged at his hair and made his eyes water. The cords spooled out of Granny's belt with a high-pitched noise – but then Josh realized that was Kiki.

"Eeeeeeeeeeeheehehehe!" She started to giggle as the cords caught them and lowered them gently to the ground beside the car. "That was great!"

Jessica was waiting at the bottom. "You okay?" Josh and Jessica chorused to each other at exactly the same time. "Of course," they both answered.

"Let's go," Granny said. "We've got a show to catch."

After a crazy, hyper-speed drive through Tokyo, Granny pulled the car up to the stage door of the TV studio. Josh smiled to himself, remembering that the last time they were in the car with Granny, she was scolding Kiki's bodyguard for driving too fast!

The rest of Team O stood outside the building, waiting to greet them. Nana gave Josh and Jessica a big grandmotherly hug. Then Kiki leaped out of the car, the skirts of her now mostly ruined dress flying behind her, to gasps of amazement from the studio technicians.

"Ayumi," someone shouted as Josh and the others followed her through into the backstage corridor. "Guess who's back!"

"Kiki? *Kiki!* Oh my, is that really you?"

"It's me," said Kiki, running up to a woman wearing a radio mic and carrying a clipboard. "Sorry I'm a little late! Do I still have a job?"

"Are you joking?" Ayumi gaped at her. "Someone tell Yoko Yay her services are not required. What *happened*? Did you escape?" she asked.

"The National Police rescued me – the thug who kidnapped me got away and I didn't even see his face!"

Out of the corner of his eye, Josh spotted Granny Murata nod ever so slightly. Kiki had picked up her lines brilliantly, for such a short in-car briefing.

"Tell me the rest as we go," Ayumi said. "Maybe we can work it into the show. In fact, I've got a *great* idea..." She started to lead Kiki down the corridor.

Kiki stopped her. "Wait – my friends!" she said, running back to Josh and the others. She shook hands with Nana, Sachiko, Nakamura and Mimasu, hugged Granny and Mr. Yamamoto, and bent down to give Josh and Jessica a kiss on the cheek. "Thank you all," she whispered.

"No problem!" Josh grinned, trying not to go bright red.

"You'll all come to the show, right?"

"Kiki, come on, we need at least ten minutes to get you into your costume," said Ayumi. "I promise they'll have the best seats in the house."

Kiki let Ayumi pull her away, and a security guard appeared and escorted Josh, Jessica and the others down a corridor full of TV equipment.

A scream and a crash made them stop in their tracks. Granny's hand went straight to her belt and Josh realized that he had already dropped into his ready stance. But then around the corner came Yoko Yay, flanked by security guards and followed by her army of squealing girls.

"You cannot do this to me!" she said, kicking out at a potted plant as she passed. "My grandfather will have something to say about this! You'll all suffer!" She tried to seize some equipment to smash, but the security guards walked her firmly towards the exit. Josh and Jessica high-fived each other as she was frogmarched away.

Josh and the others were whisked through a door

and out into a huge arena with hundreds of seats, nearly all filled. The guard found them places in a roped-off part right in the middle. A young couple passed them, carrying refreshments. Josh heard the girl say, "I wish Kiki was here. Yoko Yay's rubbish – but I suppose at least she's only presenting." Josh exchanged an enormous grin with Jessica. The audience hadn't been told! Boy, were they in for a surprise.

"Sachiko-san, thank you for the disguises," Josh said, settling down in his chair and reaching for a complimentary drink of water. "And Mimasu-san – those fold-up katana were *genius*! Although I think I might have lost mine," he added.

"Don't worry about it," said Mimasu with a smile. "I have lots of other fun toys I'd love you to try out."

Before Granny could protest a beeping sound started coming from her pocket.

"Granny!" Jessica protested. "You can't have your mobile on during the show!"

"Do you wish me to hang up on your father?" Granny asked, showing them the caller ID. She answered the phone, and chattered away in Japanese for a few seconds, then nodded. "Oh yes, they are fine, but we cannot talk long," she said, glancing at Josh. "We are just about to watch a show together." Granny winked at them. "Yes, we're getting along wonderfully. Yes? Yes, of course...I understand completely. Please give my regards to Julia." She hung up. "It looks as if your parents will be staying in Africa for a little while longer," she said. "And, so, that means you'll have to stay with me a little longer. If that is agreeable to you, that is," she asked with a smile.

Josh grinned back. *Are you kidding?* he thought. *Spending more time with my ninja granny? Best. Summer. Ever. If only we'd caught Yoshida...* It gave him the chills to think of the Yakuza and the Iron Fist still out there, causing trouble. But one day he swore the Muratas would beat the Yoshidas for good!

Suddenly the lights in the arena started to go down. A hush fell on the audience. Granny switched off her mobile phone.

A light appeared onstage. It looked as if it was being projected through rippling water. Then as the light grew brighter, Josh realized the whole stage had been turned into a river of silk that ran around three smaller stages, each set up with band equipment.

A waterfall of blue gauze was hanging in front of the centre stage.

The silhouette of a girl carrying a guitar appeared, projected onto the flowing wave of blue silk. Three guitar chords rang out, and then the lights went up, the waterfall descended, and the crowd went wild. Josh and the others all leaped to their feet in applause. Kiki grinned at them all and waved.

"Thanks, thanks, everybody!" she cried. "It feels so great to be here!"

Josh knew precisely what she meant.

Can the

**protect an international footballer from
mysterious and deadly attacks?**

Find out in

Read on for a sneak preview...

FOOTBALL FRENZY

The crowd filled the Ajinomoto Stadium with waves of noise that echoed between the huge screens showing advertisements for fizzy drinks. One of them flashed up the score: *EXTRA TIME: JAPAN 1 – 0 PORTUGAL.*

Josh leaned forward, his heart in his mouth, as out on the pitch the Portuguese striker turned on his heel and managed to get the ball past the Japanese defenders.

"No!" Kiki Chiba squealed and hunched down in the seat next to Josh, half-hiding behind her Japan scarf. The striker barrelled towards the goal with the defenders in his wake. Josh could feel the crowd around him breathing in, clutching their flags, all eyes on the white figure in the goal.

"Save it, Shini..." Josh muttered.

The striker feinted right, then sent the ball arcing towards the left side of the goal. Shinichiro Hanzo – the best player in the J League, maybe the best goal-keeper in the world – leaped like a cat, snatching the ball just before it crossed the goal line. He landed and rolled, the ball safely cradled to his chest.

The crowd went crazy as he stood up and booted the ball down the pitch to the waiting feet of a Japanese midfielder. He turned to the home fans and raised both hands in triumph.

"Go Shini! *Hai, hai, hai!*" Kiki shrieked happily, leaping out of her seat and jumping up and down.

"It's not quite over yet..." Jessica said. She was glancing from the action to her watch and back, her face full of tension. "Come on, ref, blow the whistle!"

The Portuguese and Japanese players were scrapping

over the ball in the centre circle, fighting for control...

Then the ref blew his whistle.

The crowd roared again. Kiki screamed with joy, the strength of her pop-singer lungs making Josh's ears ache.

"Come on!" she said, flinging the end of her scarf over her shoulder. "Let's go down and congratulate him!"

The twins shared a glance. "Erm...okay!"

Josh tried to look cool, casual – but it was hard to be cool and casual when he was being waved through a VIP door and into the private areas of the stadium. The place was massive, and the corridor he, Jessica and Kiki walked down felt like it would never end. Finally, they came to a lift, which took them down to *another* corridor.

As they walked, Jessica put a hand over her nose. "What's that smell?"

Josh grimaced. "I think it's...*feet*."

"Ah, here it is," said Kiki. "Locker rooms." She pushed open a swinging door, and the twins followed her through into a large room full of wide wooden benches, lockers, and rows of hooks in the walls. It was empty. "We did take a while to get here," Kiki said. "I guess they've all changed. Maybe Shini's waiting upstairs..."

"Wait," said Jessica. "Did you hear that?" She walked over to an archway in the wall. An identical room lay on the other side, and as Josh walked up behind her he heard it too – *voices*.

"*Ieie*," one of them said. "*No*. I will not."

It was Shini. Josh peered around the archway, and saw him standing with his arms folded and his shoulders hunched, glaring at a man in a large overcoat and a hat. *That's odd,* thought Josh. *It's very warm outside and even warmer down here.*

Shini looked up and saw Kiki and the twins. The other man glanced at them, though Josh couldn't see his face. Then he strode off through a door, slamming it behind him.

"Hey, Shini," Kiki said. "What was all that about?"

"Oh...nothing," Shini said, shrugging. "He was just a fan. A bit...intense. They ask you very odd things. You know."

"I do." Kiki laughed, and it seemed to brighten Shini's mood. He smiled at her, then at Josh and Jessica. Josh beamed back.

"That was amazing!" he blurted out. "The match, I mean. You were great."

"*Dōmō arigatō*." Shini grinned.

"Shini," Kiki said, "these are my friends, Josh and Jessica Murata. They're half-English, visiting from London."

"Oh really?" said Shini, still smiling. "Who will you be cheering for on Saturday?"

Josh threw a glance at his sister. Jessica shrugged – she didn't know what to say, either. "Er...I think... the best team should win," he said.

Shini laughed again. "It's a good answer! England will be tough. Neil Ash's right foot is my personal worst enemy this week."

"But England's weaker in defence now that Daniel Akimbe's out with a leg injury," Josh pointed out.

"*But*, I hear Karl Clarke is on fine form," Shini countered. Josh had to concede that one – all the football websites he'd checked said the English Captain was in better health than ever, and playing brilliantly. "This will be a great match," Shini continued. "I must admit, I am thrilled to meet them all. What club do you two support?"

"Arsenal, mostly," said Jessica. "But our mum still supports Wingate and Finchley, even though they are in, like, the *eighth* division."

"Ah, then the great 'Clarkey' is of your home team?" Shini asked.

"Yep." Josh beamed.

"English football is very physical, right?" Shini asked. Behind him, Kiki was making a big show of rolling her eyes. She had been into the match, but was now giggling at all the football geekiness. Shini didn't notice. "I hear England has a totally different style of play to the J League, and a different style of management too. Our manager at the Kashima Antlers is very strict, but I hear of English players going to lots of nightclubs."

"Yeah," Josh said. "They train hard, but the managers let them have a bit of fun, too. Well, the players would probably riot if they tried to stop them!"

Kiki started to say something, but Shini spoke

before she could. "How many games would an English team normally play in a season?" he asked. "And how do English clubs compete in the European leagues?"

"Well," Josh said, "Premier League clubs play thirty-eight matches in a season, not counting the FA Cup and the European games – the top four Premiership clubs compete in the Champion's League, and the fifth and sixth and the winner of the FA cup get to play in the Europa Cup..."

Kiki's head dropped, and she made a loud snoring sound. Josh laughed, and so did Jessica and Shini. "Sorry, Kiki," Shini said, patting her shoulder.

Kiki lifted her head, winking at Jessica. "I'm just joking."

"But England's a great place to play football, Shini," said Josh. "We've got loads of incredible stadiums, and the most dedicated fans in the world. Just look at our mum with Wingate and Finchley!"

"Shini, do not use my young friends as your personal research team," Kiki interrupted, wagging a finger at him in a mock telling-off.

"But you know I am very interested in English football," Shini said.

Josh couldn't help his eyes going wide. *Could Shini be thinking of transferring to an English club? Have I just talked him into it?* Josh wondered. *Do I get some kind of finder's fee for that?*

"Anyway," Shini continued, "how could I not want to know how the game is played in England? It is the home of football!"

"Which means it will be even better to beat them at their own game," said Kiki, with a wink at Josh and Jessica. "Sorry, guys, but it is true!"

"Not very sporting though, old thing," Shini said, attempting a comically bad English accent.

"All is fair in love and football," Kiki said, flashing him a twinkly smile.

Now it was Josh's turn to roll his eyes, but Jessica wasn't paying attention. She was staring straight at Kiki and Shini.

"Soooo," she said, "is there something you two want to tell us?"

Find out how Shini's secrets lead to more high-kicking ninja action for Josh and Jess in...

ISBN 9781409521976

Coming soon